HARBOR BLUES

CHERYL DEVENNEY

First Edition

Printed in the United States

ISBN-13: 978-0-578-54410-6
ISBN-10: 0-578-54410-5

"Harbor Blues" is dedicated to my husband, Chuck, a career law enforcement officer. I didn't plan to marry a cop. Ours was a college romance that led to him joining the police force.

Whether for good or bad, his job has always been at the center of our lives. Aside from dealing with the obvious danger and crazy hours of the job, I found that there is a bigger challenge: the badge is a formidable mistress that, more often than not, has her way.

It hasn't always been easy, but I'm glad I've stuck it out. Because behind my husband's badge, lies a heart of gold. He's been at my side through my many physical challenges, and he is completely devoted to our family. And, I might add, a terrific technical advisor to me for this book. ☺

All and all a pretty great guy!

CHAPTER 1

1997

MELANIE SWUNG HER pearl-white Mercedes coupe into her usual spot in the back of the lot. She killed her lights, and then gave a 360 degree glance around the parking lot. Satisfied that no one had seen her arrive, she stepped out and made her way to the entrance of Jack's Steak n Brew, a San Fernando Valley establishment. A place she hadn't been to in a while.

As she walked she threw her short black leather jacket on over her jeans and fluffed her shoulder-length hair. Once inside, Dean, smartly dressed as always, stepped in front of her.

Leaning in, he kissed her on the mouth, lingering until she pulled back and whispered. "Okay, Dean, what was so important you couldn't tell me on the phone? This is dangerous for me. I told you we can't see each other anymore."

"Sorry, babe." He grabbed her hand and hustled her farther into the room. "I've got an old friend that wants to meet you."

"I don't want to meet anymore of your friends."

He stopped in front of a table, where a stern-faced man sat alone. "Uh, Mel." Dean said to her as he smoothed his tie, "this is James Mah. James, this is Melanie McNeil Swain."

Melanie sighed and held out her hand. "Nice to meet you."

James cracked a smile and shook her hand. "The pleasure is definitely mine." He gestured for her to sit. "I'd like to buy you a drink."

Melanie hesitated, but then sat down. "Jimmy and I go way back. He knew your father in Pedro," "Listen you two, uh, I've got to go to the head. I'll be right back."

Melanie threw Dean a dirty look and turned to James. "No drink, thanks. Did you really know my father?"

"Yes, and I was sorry to hear about his death. He talked about you quite a bit, but I never saw you around."

She gripped the purse on her lap tighter. "You were friends?"

"I own a couple of storefronts nearby." James drained the contents of his glass. "Dean tells me you're quite the businesswoman."

"Does he?" Melanie ran her fingers over the chain purse strap and scanned the room, hoping she wouldn't see any familiar faces.

"And your husband's all right with your venture?"

Melanie gripped the chain harder. "It's never come up. Why do you ask?"

"I wanted to know a little about my new neighbor.

"What are you talking about?"

"Now that his bar belongs to you."

"I don't know that yet," she snapped.

"Oh, I assumed—"

"I hadn't talked to my father for over twenty years, Mr. Mah." She hung her purse on her shoulder. "We shouldn't assume anything."

Melanie had no intention of pursuing the subject with a stranger, and seeing no sign of Dean, she excused herself and left the building.

In the parking lot, she heard Dean following close on her designer heels. When she reached the car she turned to him. "What was that all about? Who is that guy?"

"I told you. We go way back. We've done business together on and off over the years."

"And I've told *you*. I can't chance seeing you anymore for anything. The appointment is getting close, and they're watching every move Ted and I make."

"But you really should listen to James, he—"

Ignoring his remark, Melanie slid into the driver's seat, started the car, and backed up.

"Goddammit, Mel you—"

But she didn't wait to hear anymore. And as she stepped on the gas to leave, she felt the jarring punch of Dean's fist on her back fender.

THE NEXT DAY, Melanie tried without success to put her meeting with Dean and his arrogant friend out of her mind, while she attempted to listen to her husband as he spoke at a local contractor's luncheon. Ted, assistant chief of the Los Angeles Police Department (LAPD) was in the running for the chief of police spot, soon to become vacant.

"And now," he said. "If any of you haven't had the opportunity to meet my beautiful and gracious wife, let me introduce her. Honey, please stand up. Ladies and gentlemen, Melanie Swain."

It took the sound of her name to bring her back to reality. She had sat through more of these luncheons than she cared to count, and it always helped to get lost in the world she had created for herself, unbeknownst to Ted. Luckily, she excelled at hiding her true feelings behind the prepackaged smile needed at these types of affairs. She looked as good in it as in her white, form-fitting summer business suit, stilettos, and upswept hairdo. The perfect wife of the hopeful candidate.

She completed her assignment by responding with grace to the crowd's applause and working the room, alongside Ted, as they thanked each person at the door.

When the last hand had been shaken, they made their way out to the parking lot, and he walked her to her car.

"You were great, honey." He grabbed her around the waist and attempted to plant a kiss on her lips. Instead, she turned her face, leaving him with only her cheek.

They shared an awkward moment broken, when she said, "Will you be home for dinner?"

"Yeah, see you tonight."

SHE PULLED UP to the mailbox at the base of her long driveway. The tasteful houses of her neighbors were hidden by the carefully landscaped grounds around them. When she rolled her window down to reach for her mail, a burst of hot air hit her in the face. Here at her home in the Valley, it was always about ten degrees hotter than in downtown Los Angeles, and she'd never adjusted to it despite having lived here for almost twenty years.

Living closer to the ocean again was still in their plan, but for now she and Ted saw it as politically advantageous for him to remain in the Valley. She had told him early on that if she was going to be married to a cop, he would have to work to promote to at least the rank of lieutenant. His climb to the job of top cop was more than she had bargained for.

She had done nothing that day except attend the luncheon, and still she was exhausted. She remembered when she would work late into the night, closing a deal as a commercial loan officer, and would be too wired to fall asleep. As she walked into the house from the attached garage, she heard the phone ring, but she made no attempt to answer it.

Instead, she went into the kitchen, unbuttoned her blouse, and poured herself a glass of iced tea. This first really hot day of the summer, she could've kicked herself for not thinking to set the air conditioner that morning. She grabbed a couple of extra ice cubes and rubbed them behind her ears and all over her chest, then sighed with delight as the cold water trickled down to her waistline.

Now more comfortable, Melanie listened to the message which turned out to be Ted, telling her he had finally been invited to dinner that night by one of the city commissioners, and of course he had to accept. She shook her head as she deleted the message. Before leaving the kitchen, she turned to pick up the mail on the counter and shuffled through it. When she noticed an envelope addressed to her from Henry Mattson, Attorney at Law, her heart sank, and she took a deep breath.

LATER THAT NIGHT, Ted walked into darkness when he entered the house from the garage. He fumbled around for the switch by the door, flipped it on, and gave the room a cursory look. Seeing nothing out of place, he went into the kitchen, where an empty bottle of wine and a corkscrew sat amid scattered pages on the counter. He picked them up and read, "Last Will and Testament of Benjamin H. McNeil."

When he'd read enough, he hurried up the stairs to their bedroom and found Melanie asleep in her bra and panties, curled up in a fetal position next to an empty wine glass. Only the light from the muted TV illuminated the room. Smooth jazz drifted from the speakers recessed in the ceiling.

Ted sat down next to her and rubbed the small of her back, and she stirred. "It's not as if you didn't expect this," he whispered.

"I know."

"What did you think he'd do with the bar? Leave it to a stranger?"

When she didn't answer, he put his arms around her. "We'll do what we always said we would. Sell it. Call Randy if you don't think you can handle it. He'll appreciate the listing."

———

THE DAY AFTER receiving her father's will, Melanie took her troubles with her to the gym, where she met up with her friend, Sandra. As she mounted an elliptical and Sandra took the cycle next to her, Melanie filled her friend in on the arrival of the will and her reaction to it.

"You know," she concluded, "I've suppressed my feelings about my father a long time, but last night, as I read the will, they all came flooding back." She slowed her pace on the elliptical. "The trouble is I also remembered a lot of the good things." Sighing deeply, she kicked up her speed. "I always planned to get rid of the bar as soon as possible. Now I'm not sure I'm ready."

"I'm telling you, Melanie, I wouldn't sell the place," Sandra said. "It has so many possibilities."

Melanie panted and wiped her brow with her towel. "Like what?" She couldn't imagine what Sandra meant.

"Like a nightclub."

"Oh, sure." Melanie recognized Sandra's lively imagination at work.

"Just think. You could combine your business savvy with singing on your very own stage."

"I haven't sung in years. I don't think I—"

"Sure you could. You know you'd love it."

"Who'd want to watch an old broad like me sing?"

"With that bod, and your natural good looks no one would even notice your age."

"Natural?"

"Well, a little nip and tuck merely enhances what you already have."

Melanie smiled. "Yeah, right."

Sandra stopped peddling without having broken a sweat. "Oh, come on."

"I don't know."

"Look, you've been miserable since you left the bank. You're lousy at only being the supportive wife."

"Hey, I did plenty of that supportive wife stuff a long time ago."

"That's why you deserve this. Think of all those lonely nights you spent wondering if Ted was late because he'd been shot— or because he was getting laid." Sandra continued with a grin, "Of course, in either case, bloodshed would've been involved."

Melanie nodded. "You know, it's not much different now. Ted is still not home, but now it's meetings at the Biltmore with business women who pass room keys to him."

"See?"

"I said they pass the keys to him; I didn't say he uses them."

Sandra slid off the cycle and rolled around on an exercise ball. "You had Dean. Why are you so sure he hasn't had someone else?"

"Because he loves me."

Sandra rolled her eyes. "Well, you still deserve to keep the bar."

"But he won't like it. How do I tell him?"

"Melanie, most police marriages end up a statistic, like mine. You've been married more than twenty years. That's a selling point for his campaign. He can't afford trouble now."

Sandra had a tendency to be a little over the top sometimes, and Melanie often had to rein her in. But the more she thought about her friend's suggestion, the more she remembered how singing had been her lifeline. She could recall a time when it ran a close second to breathing. In those days, the possibility of reaching millions of people with her voice trumped any monetary gain. How could I have been able to put those feelings so far behind me that I'd almost forgotten them?

They were back again now, as if she were eighteen and on the verge of the life she had dreamed of since early childhood. Despite this, Melanie knew she could never realize the career she had thrown away, but suddenly it occurred to her that owning a nightclub might give her a purpose and rejuvenate her. She knew at that moment she couldn't sell her father's bar, and she would have to find a way to tell Ted.

MELANIE HAD CALLED Ted on her way home from the gym and asked him to meet her for lunch at the LAPD Academy Cafe. He waved to her from his table at the back of the room when she arrived. She was pleased to see the usual mix of new recruits, patrol officers, detectives, and brass having lunch, as she made her way to Ted. Surely with them nearby, he'd stay composed when she broke the news to him.

After listening to him go on about a department policy issue throughout their meal, Melanie told him she wanted to reopen McNeil's Pub, but didn't mention anything about a nightclub.

"You're kidding," Ted said.

Before he could continue, the server approached them with a pitcher of iced tea and asked if they wanted refills.

Ted sat back in his chair with arms folded and foot tapping while Melanie told her she would love some, and waited for the server to pour the tea.

"Why did you bring this up here?" he asked as the server departed.

Melanie didn't answer, but exchanged glances with a lieutenant at a nearby table hoping to quell the tension in Ted's voice.

The officer gave Ted a perfunctory salute. Ted acknowledged him, turned back to Melanie with a scowl, and spoke softer. "You can't be serious about running that dump."

"My father didn't think it was a dump."

"Your father didn't have any illusions about the place."

Melanie hesitated and drew a deep breath. "I don't care. It's mine now and I can't sell it yet."

Ted grimaced, "All these years, and you've never even wanted to step foot in there."

"And now he's gone."

Ted stared down as he twisted his spoon around several times on the table. Then he looked up at her. "All right, give it a try for a while."

Melanie relaxed. "Great. Maybe I can talk Connie into coming back to tend bar and help me manage."

SCOTT SWAIN STEPPED out of his late model BMW and stood amongst a sea of black and white police cars at the LAPD South Bureau building. It had been merely two days since he had parked a similar patrol car at the end of his watch at the Devonshire Station; about an hour north in the San Fernando Valley. He loved working patrol there, but he couldn't pass up this chance to work the south end of the city, even if it meant working the detective unit in the administrative office that oversaw the four southern-most geographical areas of the LAPD. Most guys would give their right arm to work detectives this soon in their career, but Scott would rather work Southeast Patrol in the Los Angeles area known as Watts. A busy station like that served as the perfect training ground for a rookie cop.

Instead, his name had turned up on the transfer list for South Bureau Detectives. He knew why, but he tried not to think about it as he slipped his suit jacket on, covering his 9mm automatic, and the badge belted at his waist. He straightened his tie and hooked his ID card to his breast pocket before entering the South Bureau building.

A young woman at the reception desk greeted him with approval and a broad smile.

Scott reciprocated. "Hi, I'm Officer Swain. I'm looking for Detective Charlie Moore."

"Oh, hello. I've, uh—" She cleared her throat and started again. "He's been expecting you. Go on in."

Amused by her reaction to him, Scott nodded and peeked over her shoulder to the office behind her, where he spotted a man sitting at a desk behind a newspaper. He entered the office and stood in front of the desk.

"Detective Moore?"

"Yeah?"

"I'm Scott Swain, your new partner."

Moving the paper aside, Charlie peered out over his half glasses and sized him up. "No shit? You don't look much like your old man."

"No, not really."

"I expected you to."

"Everybody says I look more like my mother."

Charlie studied his dark hair and full lips. "Yeah, I see the resemblance."

"You remember my mother, too?" Scott said.

"Hell, yes. I used to love to walk into the records section and be greeted by those big ti—uh—blue eyes."

Embarrassed by Charlie's obvious familiarity with his mother, Scott winced and dismissed the comment. "How long were you at Harbor Division?"

As Charlie told him he'd been there for five years, another detective stuck his head in the door. "Yo, Moore, you finish that Johnson follow up yet?"

"Nope." Charlie turned to Scott. "Thought I'd save it for my new partner."

Scott leaned back and offered the man his hand. "Hi. I'm Scott Swain."

"Oh, right. I heard we were getting a celebrity."

The detective shook his hand. "I'm Carlisle. Wow took me fifteen years to get to homicide. But then *my* old man wasn't an assistant chief. What's a Valley guy like you doing slumming down here, anyway?"

Scott didn't want to go there and had to think fast. He glanced over at Charlie and said, "Learning from the best."

Charlie grinned. "You know, this kid may have potential."

With the detective gone, Scott pulled up a chair and sat down to ask Charlie about his caseload. But Charlie put the question off by saying they could use a couple of more detective teams and brought the subject back to Scott's father.

"So college boy, you planning to follow in Ted's footsteps?"

"I haven't decided."

"Well, either you take every squint job you can, like him," Charlie said, "or you stay in the street, because shit, you know, guys like me don't promote."

Hoping to hear some profound justification for staying a street cop rather than making rank, Scott said, "You're still doing it though."

"It's not what it used to be, but if I have to be anywhere, homicide's it. People kill each other for the damnedest reasons."

Still hopeful, Scott added, "And that fascinates you?"

"Well, let's just say it doesn't bore the shit out of me." He stood up. "Why don't we grab a cup of coffee in the break room?"

In only a few minutes with Charlie, Scott had seen a view of police work different than he'd experienced at home, or even during his brief time on patrol. And although he loved his father, and was proud of the fact he ranked directly below the chief of police, he found Charlie's career much more intriguing.

"Hell, in the old days we didn't wait for trouble to find us, we'd go out and find it." Charlie dropped some coins into the vending machine. "We didn't fool around with the small shit. We went after the guns and dope."

"What about radio calls?"

"We picked up enough to stay on the radar, but we were usually too busy jacking up a bunch of gangbangers with a carload of firepower to be the first ones to respond."

Scott took a gulp of his energy drink. "Not so easy to do these days."

"Don't I know it." Charlie sipped his coffee. "We kicked more ass and took more names back then than you youngsters will do your whole career."

Scott lapped up every word and hoped to hear more about Charlie's exploits. Instead, Charlie changed the subject.

"So you're Melanie McNeil's son?" Charlie tossed Scott the car keys. "Man, it's been over twenty years. How is she?"

"Mom's good."

Charlie pointed to the blue Chevy parked near the door and said, "Jesus, she was pretty hot stuff back then."

CHAPTER 2

1973

AS MELANIE PULLED out onto the busy streets of San Pedro, she popped an eight track tape into her car stereo and rolled back the sunroof of her 1970 VW Bug. The traffic and noise contrasted with the soothing gentle breeze of the balmy summer night, drenched by a full moon glistening over the harbor. When she glanced out her window while waiting for a traffic light, she saw several police cars parked in front of a dock, where officers attempted to break up a fistfight.

"Go get 'em, guys," she said with a smile.

A few minutes later, a guard waved her through LAPD's Harbor Station gate and into the parking lot. She hurried to the employee entrance and used her key to unlock the door. Once inside, she walked into the middle of change of watch and glanced up at the 24-hour clock which read, 2350. On her way to the records unit, where she worked the morning watch as a clerk typist, she dodged officers in blue hurrying by, and arrestees waiting in the hallway for booking.

"Smitty, wait," Melanie called to one of the officers, as he headed out to his patrol car with a shotgun and a briefcase.

"Hey, McNeil. How's my ray of sunshine in the middle of the cold dark night?"

"I'm good. Check with me before Tommy's closes, will ya? I didn't bring a lunch."

"Anything for you, babe." He clicked his tongue. "See you about 0200."

She turned around and collided head-on with another officer who instantly reached out and grabbed her arms. When she glanced up into his eyes she saw they were on her boobs. "I've always dreamed of us meeting like this," he said.

Melanie scowled at him and sighed deeply. "Hi, Earl."

Before she had a chance to secure her purse in a desk drawer, the watch commander appeared with a large board and stood it up at her work station. "Here's tonight's line-up."

"Ok, I'll get right to it."

But she didn't, because another officer appeared at the counter in front of her typewriter. "Hi, Sweetie, I'm expecting a teletype. Can you check on it for me?" Melanie went to the machine, and tore off his message. He left with it, and Charlie Moore called to her from the hallway. "Hey beautiful, I need a DR number."

She took a seat in front of the typewriter that held the report number log, looked up and saw another familiar face. "Hello Charlie."

Charlie didn't have hunk status, but his tall lean frame, baby blue eyes, and flirty smile made most of the women in the station forget he had a wife and two kids.

"This place is hopping tonight," Melanie said.

Charlie sat down in the chair opposite her and leaned over the front of the typewriter. "We've just been doing our job. Protecting ravishing creatures like you from the bad guys."

Pretending to ignore his remark, she poised her hands over the keyboard, "What have you got?"

He leaned in toward her and whispered, "A burning desire to jump this counter and take you right there."

She glanced at all the people passing by and said, "Sure. All right. We can charge admission."

"If it's privacy you're looking for, I know a place. You can tell them you're taking a break. I guarantee I'll have you back in twenty minutes."

Melanie laughed. "A whole twenty minutes?"

"Hey, ask around. Some have said twenty minutes with me is the real pause that refreshes."

"That's okay. I'll stick with my nap."

"Come on Melanie, give me—"

Melanie nodded toward a coworker walking by. "Why don't you talk to Denise?"

"We've already talked. In fact, she's talked to almost every copper here."

"She actually fell for your twenty minute line?"

"Yeah, but I had her back in ten."

Melanie shook her head and placed her fingers on the typewriter. "Who's the victim, Charlie?"

Faking pain with his hand on his heart, he said, "Me."

"You? What's the crime?"

"Battery on a police officer—by a record clerk."

MELANIE RELIEVED CAROLINE Miller from the night watch. Caroline had accomplished what many of the department's women civilian employees had made a career trying to do, she had nabbed a uniform. Caroline's husband Eric had already been married when he transferred into Harbor, but as with so many cops, his wife simply didn't understand him or the job, and when Caroline happily comforted his misunderstood ego, he had no problem leaving the wife and three kids for her.

Caroline had lucked out with Eric. Most guys just moved from one willing hopeful to the next until their wives had had enough, tossed them and their tarnished badges out, and ran for the hills to marry the first plumber or businessman they could find.

Melanie wanted no part of uniform-chasing. In fact, she usually cringed when she saw her sister clerks push flirting to the limit. Unlike them, she wasn't there to find a husband. She needed to make enough money to cut a record, and jump-start her singing career. She loved to perform, and the Los Angeles Police Department would help her dream come true.

Caroline, now six months pregnant, was tiring more easily. Melanie could see it in her posture as she stood in front of the Xerox machine making copies. The machine was right outside the office of South Traffic Division, housed at Harbor station. Through the open door to the office, she watched a motorcycle officer standing over a DUI as he administered a sobriety test.

"Blow again," he said at the top of his voice to his uncooperative drunk.

Melanie walked up to the copier, and Caroline said, "I've been trying to get these reports out for two hours. I don't want to leave them for you and Denise."

Melanie surveyed the bustling station. "Must be the full moon out there tonight."

"I know, I—" A voice from the speaker box on the wall interrupted her. "Call just came out, officer needs help, Avalon and Alameda."

The announcement could be heard throughout the station and caused an exodus of uniformed officers out the station door.

Caroline stopped copying. "That's Eric's area!" She took off for the Watch Commander's office with Melanie right behind her. They nearly ran into one of the sergeants on his way out.

"Who is it?" Caroline squealed.

"5A15. Shots fired. Officer down. It sounded like Ted Swain on the radio."

A look of terror came over Caroline's face. "Eric," she cried.

Melanie wrapped her arms around her, but Caroline pulled away. "I have to go to him."

"All right," the watch commander said. "Wait. I'll find somebody to drive you to Harbor General."

Melanie didn't hesitate. "I'm going with you."

THE WOMEN WALKED into pandemonium when they arrived at the emergency room. Eric had already gone to pre-op to be prepped for surgery, and it took Caroline over half an hour to find out if his injuries were life threatening. In the meantime, Melanie located a nurse and insisted she put them in a room away from the onslaught of reporters surrounding Caroline. Concerned for the baby, Melanie tried to keep her as calm as possible while they waited for what seemed like forever.

Once they learned Eric had only been shot in the arm, they relaxed a bit. But there still remained some chance the surgery would not restore full use of it, and they waited with family and friends through a long and troubling night to hear the outcome. Ted, Eric's partner, had been there a few minutes and wanted to stay, but had been hustled off for questioning by detectives and Internal Affairs. After the surgery, when Eric and Caroline were resting comfortably, Melanie hitched a ride back to the station with Smitty and his partner.

WITH THE SUNRISE as a backdrop, the black-and-white pulled up behind Melanie's VW. She thanked the officers and walked to her car, where she stopped to yawn and rub one eye before unlocking the door. She threw her purse on the passenger seat, took a tissue out of her pocket, and wiped the dew off the windshield. As she slid behind the wheel, a voice from behind surprised her.

"How is he?"

She turned her head. "Oh, Ted. I didn't see you there." She took a deep breath. "He's hurting, but they say his arm is going to be fine."

"Good."

Melanie studied him. "You look beat. They finished with you?"

"For now. I've got to talk with the department shrink later today."

Melanie nodded and yawned again.

"You've had a pretty rough night yourself. Have you eaten anything?"

"Do ten cups of coffee and a Snickers bar count?"

He chuckled. "How about some breakfast?"

"That sounds good." She tugged at her rumpled ribbed sweater and smoothed her bell-bottom pants. "But I'm a mess."

"You look good to me," he said.

After a moment's uncertainty, Melanie removed her purse from the passenger seat. "Come on. Get in."

He ran around to the other side of the car and jumped in. Ten minutes later, with more light in the sky, they drove past Ports O'Call Village and pulled up in front of McNeil's Pub.

Ted peered at the building "I don't think this place is open for breakfast."

"It will be as soon as I unlock the door."

Once inside the bar, Melanie led Ted into the kitchen. She fried up some ham and eggs and put out some cherry Danish she'd bought fresh the day before. They made small talk while she cooked; chatting about the people they worked with at Harbor Station. Ted didn't share what he had experienced the night before, and that pleased Melanie, because she really didn't want to hear about it. In fact, she welcomed the distraction cooking provided, lest her mind dwell on what she had been through with Caroline and Eric.

They ate quickly and in silence for almost ten minutes, both famished in body and spirit. Ted put his fork down and lit a cigarette. "You know, I used to come to this bar when I was in the service. I don't remember seeing you here, though."

"Oh, I was around, but I was too young to wait tables."

"How old are you now?"

"Twenty-one."

Ted scanned his surroundings. "Have you always lived here?"

"As long as I can remember. Mom and Dad met while he was stationed at Long Beach in the Navy and bought this place afterward."

"And your Mom?"

"She died when I was twelve."

"That's rough, I'm sorry"

Melanie stared off into space and nodded.

"And what made you want to work for the LAPD?"

"I didn't intend to. I applied for a job with the City of Los Angeles and that's where the openings were. I need a regular paycheck until I can support myself with my singing."

"A singer, huh?"

"Yeah. I know it's a long shot, but it's what I've always wanted to do."

"No, I think it's terrific. You should go for it."

"You've haven't even heard me sing," she said with a smile, but felt a twinge of embarrassment when he grinned back. So she changed the subject, "Did you always want to be a cop?"

"Heck, no. All I was looking for was a good time when I came back from 'Nam. But that only lasted until I'd spent all of my separation money and started getting desperate. I saw an ad in the paper, and here I am."

"Somehow, I envisioned you having some noble reason. Like saving the world from itself, or something."

Ted laughed and said, "Is that how I come off?"

Melanie shrugged.

He took a drag of his cigarette and said, "I'm going to have to work on that."

"No, don't," she pleaded. "I think you have a nice way about you."

Ted's eyes widened. "Does that mean you'd go out with me sometime?"

"No."

"Oh."

She saw his chin drop and added, "Don't take it personally. I don't date any policemen."

"Why not?"

"Lots of reasons, but last night is the best one I can think of at the moment."

They both appeared relieved when her father, a bald-headed man in his fifties, walked in yawning.

"Well, good morning,' he said at the sight of Ted sitting at the table with Melanie.

"Good morning, Daddy." Melanie rose and kissed him on the cheek. "I'm sorry if we woke you." She poured him a cup of coffee and set it on the table.

"Time I got up anyway." He took a seat in front of the coffee cup, but kept his eyes on Ted.

"This is Ted Swain, a new officer at the station. Ted this is my father, Benny McNeil."

"How do you do Mr. McNeil."

Benny hesitated, acting a little confused.

"Dad?"

"Oh, nice to meet you son. I'm just a little surprised, that's all. Melanie doesn't usually bring anybody home from work."

"This was different. Ted was involved in a shooting last night, and—"

"No kidding," Benny said. "Did you get him?"

"Ah, yes sir. We did."

"Good." Benny sipped his coffee.

Ted, checked his watch, and stood up. "I'd better get going. I've got a long drive."

"Where's home?" Benny said.

"North Long Beach."

"You had any sleep lately?"

"About twenty four hours ago."

"You're welcome to stay her."

Melanie couldn't believe what Benny had said. "Oh," She added," He probably would rather go home. After all he—"

But before she could finish, Ted smiled at her and said that he'd like to stay.

Benny wasted no time. "Come on, I'll show you the room."

Melanie shook her head as she watched Benny lead Ted down the hallway.

———

MELANIE HAD DIFFERENT days off at Harbor Station every month, and she liked the flexibility, because in addition to working there and for her father, she belonged to a rock band. The members had formed the group while in high school and asked Melanie and her friend, Karen, to join them. When she took the job at the PD, the group members weren't happy. They complained she had sold out to the "establishment."

She couldn't deny that there was some truth to that. No one at Harbor station was aware of her singing gigs, because she didn't want the department to know she spent her days off with a rock band and its audiences, which were often high on a variety of illegal substances. It had become a balancing act for her to maintain living in both worlds, but it was worth it. She also knew that the band didn't have much choice, but to accept her job at the PD. She was their star attraction.

"That was a great audience," Melanie said coming backstage.

"And you look great," Karen said, as she eyed Melanie's black leather mini skirt and low cut flowered blouse.

Melanie smiled in thanks, as she gathered her belongings to leave. "We should've done another number."

"One encore's enough," Mike, the bearded bass player said. "That's what keeps 'em comin' back for more."

Pete twirled his drumsticks. "Hey, you were pretty awesome tonight."

"And," Mike added, "you were with us all the way."

"Yeah," Melanie said, "In spite of you changing the harmony on that last number."

Pete raised his hands to declare his innocence. "That was Mike's idea," he said, "I was afraid we were going to lose you."

Mike inhaled his cigarette and let it out. "Hell, I knew she'd maintain."

Melanie grinned and kissed his cheek.

"You sure you won't go to Derek's with us?" Mike asked. "He always has nothing but the finest shit."

It was a familiar scenario backstage after every performance. As usual, Melanie refused his invitation and said goodnight.

THE FOLLOWING WEEK, Melanie performed solo at McNeil's before her shift at the station. She often sang in-between waiting tables. The bar bustled with activity that night. She sat on a stool at the end of the bar counter, with eyes closed, oblivious to the clientele around her. Ted watched her from the bar as Connie poured drinks, and Charlie, who sat in a booth alone, appeared mesmerized by her sexy voice. Melanie met Charlie's gaze as she finished the song and walked up to his table.

"Never saw you here off-duty," she said.

"Thought I'd like to see you in your own surroundings."

"Really."

"Actually, Ted over there, told me you were a pretty good singer, so I wanted to see for myself."

"So what do you think?"

"He was wrong—You're great."

"Thank you."

"Anybody in the business heard you?"

Melanie sat across from him. "Not that I know of."

"You really should get a hold of someone."

"I'm trying to save enough money for a demo tape."

Charlie hesitated and rubbed his chin. "Ya know, I worked security for a big shot record producer's wedding last year. Maybe I could give him a call."

Melanie's face lit up. "Are you kidding? Could you?"

"Sure."

"That would be so great. If I could just audition, I know I could—"

"So why don't you meet me later," he said as he stroked her hand, "and we can talk about it."

"All ri—," Melanie began then retracted her hand. "Uh, no thanks. That's okay. I've had a couple of those offers already."

"You don't think I would—"

Before he could finish, a drunk at a neighboring table grabbed Melanie's arm. "C'mere sweetheart."

Melanie turned toward him. "What else can I get for you, Stan?

"How about a little company with our drinks?"

Melanie yanked her arm from his grasp and pointed to a group that had just taken a table. "I see some fellows over there that look pretty thirsty."

But Stan was determined to detain her. "Hell, they can wait. We've been here longer."

"Just let me take their order and I'll be right back."

But Stan again grabbed her arm and dragged her toward him. This time she lost her balance and she fell into his lap.

"Now this is the kind of service I'm talking about," he said.

Before she could draw herself up, Ted appeared jerking her up from Stan's lap and pushing Stan over in his chair. Melanie tugged at Ted's arm, but he had already jumped on Stan and grabbed him by the collar. "You got your drink. That's all she's selling."

Stan bolted up and threw a punch at Ted's head, which Ted easily blocked and then executed a blow to Stan's gut. But before Ted could applaud himself, Stan's friend jumped Ted from behind, and Ted struggled to throw him off his back. Charlie, who had been watching from the sidelines, finally joined in and yanked the guy off Ted and threw him to the floor.

Within seconds there was a free-for-all in the bar. Melanie fumed as she and Connie watched glasses fly off the tables, shattering on the floor, and chairs were tossed from one end of the small room to the other. She had the phone in her hand, ready to call the station, when Ted grabbed Stan by the shoulders and shoved him into a chair. Before Stan could retaliate, Ted pulled his police badge out of his pocket, flashed it in Stan's face and yelled, "Police! That's enough!"

The rest of the fighters turned toward Ted and stared in disbelief. Charlie then climbed onto a chair and lifted his badge above his head.

"Now get the hell out of here before we book your drunken asses," Ted said.

"Since when's this place a hangout for fuckin' pigs?" Stan wiped his bloody mouth on his sleeve and made his way out the door with his buddies in tow.

Charlie offered his hand to Ted, "Good job, Swain."

"Thanks for the assist."

"Hell, I enjoyed it. Haven't been in a bar fight in months."

Melanie overheard them, and fueled by her rage, started to straighten up the mess at once. Some of the regulars stayed to help clean up and guzzle a few more drinks to help numb their wounds. Ted and Charlie seemed unaware of them.

"I don't think they'll be back," Ted boasted.

"Shit, no. Did you see the look on that guy's face when—"

"I could've handled that myself," Melanie said with disgust, "and without trashing the room."

Ted said. "I'm sorry, but that guy was all over you."

"It didn't call for the militia, for crying out loud."

"I guess I shouldn't have pulled my badge, but he was an asshole."

"That asshole's money is as good as anybody's. What the hell are you trying to do, put us out of business?"

Ted kicked a cigarette butt around on the floor as she spoke.

"When my father invited you to live here, he wasn't looking for a resident bouncer."

Melanie took a breath and continued. "And I don't need you for a bodyguard."

Then, as Charlie edged toward the door, Melanie yelled toward him, "And you. What are you doing here? Why don't you go home to your wife?"

MELANIE HAD WALKED into another busy shift at the station, right after the fiasco at the bar. At the end of watch, all she wanted to do was go home and crawl into bed when she got off that morning. But she looked at her gas gauge dial, pointing to empty.

"Dammit," she said.

The OPEC (the Organization of Petroleum Exporting Companies) crisis had made gas rationing necessary. She had remembered that her license plate ended in 3: an odd number. Today was an "odd" day at the gas station, and if she didn't fill up now, she'd have to wait two days. She sighed and pulled up to the back of a line flowing out into the street.

Nearly an hour later, she arrived home, and her father had breakfast waiting for her.

"This is great, Dad. Thanks," Melanie said, as she poured syrup on her pancakes. "All I had to eat during the night was a dried-out burrito from the vending machine."

"You're very welcome. By the way, I saw Connie before he closed up last night. He told me about the donnybrook."

"Yeah. Sorry about that. It shouldn't have gone that far. Ted and Charlie overreacted to Stan's advances, and before I knew it, they came out swinging."

Benny smiled and took a swig of coffee. "There've been plenty of times I'd have liked to take a poke at Stan myself."

"Dad, if you had beat up everybody who made a pass at me since I reached puberty, we wouldn't have any customers."

Benny nodded. "You know why it happened, though, don't ya?"

"Yeah. If I've learned anything in my time at the PD, it's that coppers are issued egos with their badges."

"That may be true, but Ted has it bad for you, ya know."

She nibbled a piece of bacon. "He's made that pretty clear. And it hasn't helped that you invited him to stay here."

"I did that for you."

"For me?"

"He's a good guy. Better than the drunken sailors you meet here. And I know he'd take care of you after I'm gone."

Melanie plunked her napkin in her plate. "First of all, you're not going anywhere for a long time; second, I don't want to marry a cop, and most importantly, I'm not attracted to him that way."

CHAPTER 3

1997

SCOTT SPENT SATURDAY morning doing his laundry, and he didn't mind it at all. He enjoyed having his own washer/dryer in the two bedroom bungalow he rented in San Pedro. His former apartment complex, had him running back and forth to the community laundry. Now he could throw a load in and sprawl out on his sofa to watch a game on TV until the buzzer called him.

He loved the weather, too. Living only a few blocks from the ocean, he found the moderate temperature had it all over the extreme heat and cold of the Valley. Though it was June, the seventy-degree temp and mild ocean breeze energized him. In fact, he would have liked to have taken a bike ride.

Unfortunately, he had promised his mother he would meet her and Connie at McNeil's Pub. He knew she needed moral support since she hadn't spoken to Connie in years, and didn't know what his reaction would be to her new plan. He had seen Connie at Benny's funeral, and Connie hadn't changed. Though long dry-docked, he was always the salty sailor at heart, traveling light and ready to leave at four bells' notice if bitten by wanderlust. But he always came back to McNeil's and had been there as long as Scott could remember.

Scott had many fond memories of those times as a child when his father would take him to visit Benny. But in spite of the fact he had been almost as close to Connie as he had been to his grandfather, he wasn't sure whether Connie would take Melanie up on her offer. Regardless, he was happy she had decided not to sell his grandfather's bar.

MELANIE HAD DRIVEN over an hour from her Valley home. Now, within minutes from McNeil's Pub, her heart raced at the thought of seeing Connie again. She knew he had been disappointed she hadn't attended her father's funeral, but she had never been able to tell him why. She only hoped he wouldn't use that as a reason for turning down the job.

As she neared the San Pedro exit, she caught a glimpse of the new Harbor Station to her left, along with rows of container ships lining the harbor. The sight prompted her to lower her window, open her sunroof, and welcome the cool breeze as it washed over her face. She flipped off the air conditioner, turned the music up on her seventies CD, and took a deep whiff of the ocean air. She hadn't realized how much she had missed the harbor area.

She smiled when she saw Scott's car as she pulled around the back of the bar. Thank goodness he agreed to be here today. He would help smooth over her rough spots with Connie, and she always enjoyed spending time with her son.

She found Scott in front of the locked building. They embraced, and he wasted no time telling her what Charlie Moore had said about her.

"I remember Charlie very well," Melanie said with a smile.

"Well, he sure had the hots for you. In fact, so did some of the other old-timers I've talked to."

She pretended to be insulted. "Don't sound so surprised."

"All I know is, I expected Dad's reputation to follow me to South Bureau, and instead you're all they talk about."

"Knowing cops, their stories are probably as inflated as their egos," she said as she fumbled in her purse for the keys.

"Sure, sure."

Melanie laughed. "Those old guys are just happy to remember what it was like to have horns—and hair."

She finally found the key and turned it in the lock. When they entered the dimly-lit bar, they both stopped laughing, as if on cue. The familiar scent of mildew and stale beer still lingered in the air, and the old fishing paraphernalia hung among the beer signs on the wall as they had last seen them. Melanie found her way to the light switch and turned on the overhead lights.

She eased over to the bar counter and stepped behind it. On-the-rocks glasses, coated in dust, sat in the sink. She hit the no sale button on the circa 1960's cash register, and the empty drawer flew out causing her to jump back in surprise. When she reached for the tap of a beer keg, it came off in her hand. She turned her attention to an old fishing hat hanging on a hook, and she leaned over to stroke it. The sight of the rundown space broke her heart, because she knew it hadn't become that way in the few short months since Benny had been gone.

Scott saw her blink back tears and tried to break the mood. "This is a great old place." He hopped up on a bar stool and said with a grin, "How many sailors do you figure have occupied this seat over the years?"

"Lots." Melanie lowered her eyes and came out from behind the bar as Scott moved to one of the tables carved with several names.

"Remember any of these people?" Scott asked.

Melanie went to the table and ran her fingers over the names, stopping at one that read, "Stan."

Scott waited for her to answer him, but the look on her face told him he wasn't going to hear about Stan, or anyone else on her mind. So he hung back as he watched her wander from the bar toward her father's apartment, situated down the hall.

Inside the comfortable space, she took a deep breath as she gazed around the room from picture to picture of herself at various ages. Her eyes stopped at a pose of her and her father on the pier in front of their small sloop, and she smiled. Forcing herself to look away, she noticed a windbreaker on the back of the couch. She walked over to it and ran her fingers over the worn and wrinkled material.

Her chest tightened and her chin trembled as she shuffled into the kitchen where she spotted a coffee cup with a spoon in it, next to the coffee maker. Benny had always left it there each night, waiting for the next morning's brew. Above the cup hung a pair of dingy curtains framing a dusty window, and Melanie peeked through it at the stairway leading to the upstairs apartment that had been her home before marrying Ted.

A few minutes later, Melanie stepped out the front door behind Scott, in time to see Oscar "Connie" Conroy climb out of his gold Buick Skylark. His silhouette, complete with sailor's cap, and cigar protruding from his mouth, seemed so familiar to her. Yet she could see how the years had left their mark. He moved slower, favoring his right leg, and his face, always tanned and somewhat weathered, was now leathery and deeply lined. When their eyes met, she saw the broad smile she remembered so well, and as he opened his arms to her she suddenly had a sense of well-being she hadn't felt for quite some time.

"Connie, it's so good to see you," she said pressing into his shoulder.

He pulled back, now holding her at arm's length. "Still the looker," he said with admiration. "I knew you would be."

"Thanks. You look terrific, too."

He turned toward her son. "Hey, Scott,"

"How you doing, Connie?"

Connie pinched Scott's cheek, then said to Melanie, "Your father thought the world of this boy." His voice softened. "But he never understood why you wouldn't come down with him and Ted."

Melanie shrugged and changed the subject. "Thanks for handling all the funeral arrangements. I really couldn't be there after all this time."

"I'd do anything for Benny, and I always told him I'd keep an eye on you if he wasn't around, so here I am."

"I'm glad, because I have something to ask you. Come on inside."

After hearing her idea, Connie sat back in the booth and rubbed his chin. "I don't know. This place ain't the moneymaker it used to be."

"That's okay. I'm not doing it for the money," Melanie said.

Connie sighed and took a long look around the room, "Old Ben must be turning over in his grave." He turned to Melanie. "Oh, what the hell. I've kinda missed standing behind that bar. I'll do it."

THE PLACE REQUIRED some fixing up before she could welcome customers, but Ted refused to help, because he wanted to distance himself from the bar while awaiting the city council's choice for chief. Melanie planned to hire a building contractor she and Ted had used in the past. But Scott, Connie and Sandra insisted on helping her do the work, which involved a lot of cleaning, some light carpentry, and painting.

Three weeks into the job, as Connie stood in the storage room inventorying the liquor, and Scott finished up some last minute chores, a dark haired young woman walked through the opened back door. She walked down the hallway and stopped at the entrance to the bar, where Scott stood on a ladder changing a light bulb.

She cleared her throat and waited.

Scott found himself peering into her low-cut tank top, which he followed up to the biggest brown eyes he'd ever seen. "Oh, I didn't hear you come in." He stepped down off the ladder.

"Sorry if I startled you. I saw the back door open and came in. I guess I should not have—"

She spoke with a pretty thick accent, which he guessed to be western European. "No. It's all right," he said. "What can I do for you?"

"I saw the ad in the paper for a bartender and thought I could help you."

"I'm sure you could," he said under his breath.

"Pardone?"

"Oh, uh, nothing."

"Is the job still available?"

"Yes, uh, yes it is. It sure is—" He trailed off deep in thought.

She waited a few awkward seconds. "Well, is there a form I should fill out, or something?"

Finally returning to earth, Scott called toward the back-room, "Connie, someone is here to apply for the bartender job."

Connie came out of the storage room, introduced himself, then said, "What's your name, young lady?"

"Adriana Dimakos."

"Dimakos, huh? Where have you worked?"

"Mostly in Greece, but I was at a place like this in Monterey before coming here."

"What brings you here?"

"My cousin invited me to visit him. He lives in Long Beach."

"You got a work permit?"

"Sure," Adriana said, searching through her purse. "Oh, I must have left it at home."

Connie frowned and looked at Scott's disappointed face. "Well—wait here. I'll get you an application. You can bring the permit in later."

With Connie gone, Scott and Adriana eyed each other. Finally Adriana said, "You worked here long?"

"Uh, no. I, um, I'm just helping my mother out. She owns the place. It's not open yet. Not until next week."

"It's too bad you don't work here. But you'll come by a lot, no?"

Scott smiled, "That could be arranged."

Connie returned with the form. "Here it is."

Adriana took a few minutes to enter her information, then placed the application on the bar.

"We'll let you know in a few days," Connie said as he picked it up. "Thanks for coming in."

Adriana grimaced and said, "Thank you very much."

Scott led her to the front door, winked and said, "Don't worry. I have a lot of influence with the owner."

Adriana left smiling, and Scott joined Connie in the storage room. "Nice girl, huh?"

"All right, I guess. Rather have a guy behind the bar."

SCOTT HAD USED all of his days off for the month to help Melanie prepare the bar for opening, so he couldn't stop by again until a week after Adriana had applied for the bartender job. He located his mom alone going over some of his grandfather's accounts, and setting up a new computer accounting system. There wasn't anything left for Scott to do, but stand in the middle of the room, surrounded by Benny's vibe.

A knock on the door caused him to jump. He could see the silhouette of a woman through the window. He opened the door wide enough to stick his head out and hear Adriana call out, "Kalimera."

He smiled broadly and opened the door. "Hello. How are you? Are you here to work?"

"I did not get a call from your manager. Did he hire someone else?"

"I don't know. I haven't been here since the day you came in. I assumed he hired you." He started toward the back office, then said, "Wait here a minute."

Scott stuck his head into Melanie's office. "Mom, what's up with the bartender situation?" he said. "I don't understand. Connie and I met a perfectly good candidate last week. Didn't he mention her?"

"No, he only said that he was still looking."

Scott walked into the office. "Well, personally I've seen enough. This woman is hot."

Melanie smirked. "Maybe her references weren't so hot."

"Well she's here, and I don't know what to tell her."

Melanie went to Connie's desk and shuffled through some applications. "What's her name?"

"Adriana something. It starts with a "D.""

Melanie found her name and read the application. "Looks pretty good to me, but I don't see any notes from Connie."

"Why don't you come out and meet her, and see what you think?"

Melanie took the application and followed Scott out to the bar. One look at Adriana told her why Scott wanted to have this girl around. She had to admit it wouldn't hurt to have somebody like her behind the bar. She'd be sure to rejuvenate the clientele at old McNeil's Pub. Melanie told her to report on Friday morning to help them set up for opening night.

After walking Adriana out, Scott came back to Melanie with a gleam in his eye. "Perfect, isn't she?"

"I can give you two good reasons why you think so," Melanie said.

"Not fair. I think she'll give our bar a real international flavor." He leaned over and kissed her on the cheek.

"Uh, huh," she said with a smile.

"Gotta go. See ya later."

"Bye, sweetheart."

Scott walked toward the door as James Mah entered carrying a potted plant. They acknowledged each other, and James presented the plant to Melanie.

"Well, Melanie, it looks like your father came through."

Surprised to see him, she said, "James, isn't it?"

"Yes, and I'd like to personally welcome you to the neighborhood."

"Thank you." She put the plant on the bar.

"So what are your plans?"

"Plans?"

"For this place. I can't imagine you intend to keep it."

"As a matter of fact, I do."

"What would someone in your position want with this?"

"It is where I grew up."

"I realize that your father's death is still very fresh, but when you've gotten past some of the emotion, you'll be able to accept a more logical disposition of the bar."

"What are you talking about?"

"I want this property, and I'm prepared to pay you a more-than-generous sum for it."

"But I don't—"

"You may change your mind when you see my offer." He handed her his card. "Think about it. I'll be in touch."

Melanie glanced at the amount scribbled on the business card. It was quite a generous offer, considerably higher than the going rate for property in the area. Definitely tempting. But she had really enjoyed the past couple of months preparing to open McNeil's again, and she had to do it.

Sandra had been right. She needed this; something of her own to sink her time and talents into, and no amount of money could take the place of that. She felt a little guilty though, because she didn't plan to tell Ted. If he knew how much money she had turned down, he wouldn't understand.

SCOTT'S CASELOAD DOUBLED the next week, and he hadn't had a chance to get by McNeil's since it opened. According to his Mom, things were going okay, but he had to see for himself, so he stopped by Monday evening after work. When he arrived, he saw Connie sitting out in front smoking a cigar.

"Hey, Connie, how's business?" Scott said.

"See for yourself. Your Mom's inside."

Scott beamed when he walked into the familiar sights and sounds of the bar he remembered as a kid. Though the jukebox blared, the music served only as a backdrop to the rousing chatter of pool balls clapping, and glasses clinking. It only took him a minute to find Melanie, clothed in her Saks Fifth Avenue outfit. He was used to his mother standing out in a crowd, but she looked out of place among the tee shirts and jeans in the bar.

Melanie, who sat in a booth across from Sandra, waved Scott over. After nodding a greeting to Sandra, he scooted in next to his mother.

"I'm beat."

Melanie pushed his hair out of his eyes. "Busy week, huh?

Scott ran his fingers through his hair. "Dad know you're here tonight?"

"I'll tell him tomorrow. I wasn't in the mood for a lecture on self-defense. The last time I came down here, he had me packing a 9mm."

A commotion drew their attention to a ruckus in the pool room, where one gangbanger had another pinned to the table with a knife secreted between their bodies. Scott reached into the holster under his jacket and began to get up, but Melanie grabbed his arm and pulled him back into his seat. He let out a sigh, but remained seated and waited several seconds for the gangsters to separate and go back to their game.

"I hope you still have that gun with you," Scott said.

Melanie nodded.

"Let's hope the new club will bring in a classier clientele," Sandra said.

Scott squinted. "Club?"

Sandra swallowed hard and apologized with a glance at Melanie for letting the cat out of the bag. Melanie put her hand out and gestured to Sandra inviting her to explain.

"Your mother is going to remodel this place into a nightclub, and be the star singing attraction."

"Well, I don't know about the singing," Melanie said," but I am going to remodel. In fact, don't say anything to dad yet, but I talked to a restaurant consultant yesterday for some ideas, and this place is going to look so great. We could use the existing bar, but we'll have tables over…"

Adriana interrupted them, and Scott's face lit up with delight.

"Ya, Scott, you haven't been here for a while."

"We've been stacked up with cases the past couple of weeks.

"Oh, you work too hard," she scolded him.

He shrugged. "It's the job."

She reached out for him, "Come."

He threw a puzzled look at Melanie, who nodded. Adriana grabbed his forearms and pulled him up toward the small dance area near the jukebox. He followed her lead and pressed his chest against hers, with movements mimicking foreplay to the beat of the bluesy music. Captivated by her, he didn't hear the crowd cheering him on.

It wasn't until Adriana stopped, kissed him on the cheek, and left him standing there in a daze, that he realized they had an audience. He responded by dropping to his knees. He stretched his arms out toward her with the palms of his hands up and wiggled his fingers toward himself. With no response from her, he fell forward to the floor, as if in defeat, and the group around him laughed.

Melanie and Sandra had left for home a few minutes later. Now nearing closing time, Scott sat watching Adriana work the bar, mixing her brand of allure with every drink she poured; exuding sexuality simply by the way she fingered each bottle, glass, and stirrer. He'd never seen anything like it. The customers couldn't take their eyes off her, and neither could he.

Connie walked behind the bar with a couple of bottles of booze and put them in the rack with the others. Adriana spoke over her shoulder at him. "Okay if I take a little break?"

He saw Scott sitting on the stool in front of her, and said, "Looks like you could use one."

She walked outside and Scott followed.

"It's warm in there tonight," she said as she lit a cigarette.

"I noticed." He nodded toward the cigarette. "Aren't you worried about your health?"

"You take bigger risks every day at work."

He shrugged.

"Well, I think you're very brave to do what you do."

"Some people think it's pretty stupid, not brave."

"What do you think?"

"I don't. I've always known that it's what I wanted to do."

"And what about your girlfriend? What does she think."

"She thought I'd change my mind after college, and when I didn't, she boogied."

She squinted. "Translate, please."

"Left. She broke up with me."

"Oh, too bad for you." She winked. "But good for me."

"Oh, yeah?" He reached out to her, but she jerked, dropped her cigarette to the ground, and covered it with her shoe.

"I better go help Connie close," she said, and hurried inside.

Shit, shot down twice in one night. He was glad no one had seen the stupid look burning on his face. He must have read her wrong. Well, after all, she was a foreigner. Maybe he needed a different approach.

CHAPTER 4

1997

MELANIE KNEW SHE needed to tell Ted about her plan for the bar. She had put off telling him about it as long as she could. The contractor had threatened to start another job before hers if he couldn't get started soon. She rehearsed her speech several times, and set the scene for a cozy dinner at home with candles and Ted's favorite meal, but while arranging some flowers on the table, the phone rang.

It was Ted saying he wouldn't make it home for dinner again. She had no choice, but to try and catch him at breakfast, even though he wasn't his most agreeable in the morning. But he left early the next day, and something came up every day that week. Before she knew it, Thursday had arrived.

SCOTT SHOWED UP at the bar that night, but spent most of his time talking to Melanie about the remodel, and what Ted's reaction would be. Connie had the night off, and Scott had decided to play it cool and keep his distance from Adriana, so he hadn't said more than a few words to her. After they locked up, Melanie called for Adriana, but got no answer.

"She's probably in the head," Scott said.

Melanie went off to find her but came right back to report no sign of her in the backroom.

"I'll check outside."

He checked out back, but didn't find her, so he went around the side of the building to the front. There he noticed her silhouette in the shadows along with a man, holding her arms and shaking her.

Scott called out, "Adriana? Are you out here?"

With no answer, he rushed toward the twosome just in time to see the man's face as he ran off.

Scott embraced her for a moment. "Are you all right?"

"Yes."

"Who was that guy?"

"He said he had to talk to me."

"About what?"

Melanie interrupted. "Everything all right?"

"Yes," Adriana assured her.

As they walked back into the bar, Scott explained, "Some guy was harassing her."

"A customer?" Melanie said with concern.

"No," Adriana said.

Scott turned to Adriana. "Did you know him?" Scott picked up that she wasn't anxious to tell him about this guy. So when she nodded, he jumped all over her. "From where? What's his name?"

"Easy, Scott," Melanie said.

Adriana lowered her head and shifted her feet. "His name is Marco," He's uh, helping me find my father, and he wants more money."

"Your father is here? What's his name?" She wasn't talking fast enough to suit Scott.

She didn't say a word, but handed him a tattered picture of a handsome man in his late twenties.

"Maybe you'd better explain to us why you—" Scott showed Melanie the picture, and she froze.

"Mom, what's the matter?"

Melanie still didn't speak.

"Do you know him?" Adriana asked.

A dazed Melanie said, "What?"

"Who is he?"

"I just remember him, that's all."

Scott's interrogation skills kicked in. "From where?"

"It was a long time ago. Come on, let's get out of here."

Always the detective, he said, "Maybe you can remember something that could lead us to him."

1973

MCNEIL'S WAS HOPPING that night. Melanie had to squirm around the booths, tables, and people while trying not to drop her drink-laden tray on someone's head or lap. She walked up to a table of four charter boat fishermen and placed drinks in front of each of them.

"Sorry it took so long, guys."

"It was worth the wait," said a bald fellow, with a wink.

Melanie smiled, but only had eyes for one of them; a ponytailed Italian with a cropped beard and Romanesque features. She leaned into him and said, "Haven't seen you for a while."

"We just docked."

"Well, welcome back."

He handed her some money and said, "Thank you. Keep the change."

Fanning the bills, she said, "That's pretty generous."

"You're the first young lady I've seen in quite a while. Keep it."

"Okay, if you say so." Melanie said, beaming, and continued with her work.

At the end of her shift, Melanie walked out the backdoor of the bar and stood in the darkness for a moment. She crept toward her apartment and climbed the stairs. Before she could open her door, someone grabbed her arm.

She turned to face Enzo Mancini, the man who had given her the big tip. Her heart fluttered and she threw her arms around him and kissed him long and hard. They held their embrace as they moved inside, pulling and tugging off each other's clothes until they fell naked onto the bed. After the conflagration of their initial moments in the room, Enzo slowed their pace with soft whispers into her ear while caressing her face. His fingers made their way to her nipples as his lips moved along her body, and she succumbed to the sensations.

After they had satisfied one another, they held each other in silence. Then Melanie reached up and stroked his beard. "You were gone so long. I thought maybe you weren't coming back."

"I had an emergency at home."

"Why didn't you phone me?"

"Didn't you get my message?"

"No."

"I gave a letter to Sergio for you."

"I never got it."

Enzo sat up. "That son of a bitch. I let him use my boat, and he couldn't even do this for me?"

She checked her watch. "It's almost eleven. Time for me to get ready for work."

"Why don't you call in sick?"

"I can't. I'm alone in the unit tonight."

Enzo leaned over and caressed her face. "Ti amo."

"I love you too."

Before that night, Melanie had been seeing Mancini for several months. It started out as a very casual thing, but she soon fell hard for the handsome foreigner. Of all the guys she had dated or had met in the bar, he won her over. It happened the first time he'd walked into McNeil's. Despite his rugged exterior, well-carved face, and full lips, his quiet eyes were a window to his sensitive soul. He had captured more than her heart, and inviting him into her bed had changed her. Besides her singing, Mancini had become the most important thing in her life, and she lived for his arrivals in port; despite her father's disapproval.

IT HAD BEEN several weeks since Melanie had seen Enzo, He had promised he would be back in town that evening but had not shown up. She arrived at the station in a lousy mood. As she sat at the teletype machine to run some DMV information, she tried to tell herself there must be a good reason. A few minutes later, Ted leaned into the records unit window and called to her.

"What's up? she asked as she walked to the window.

"Got a minute?"

"Sure," she answered and waited for him to continue. When he didn't, she said, "Well?"

"Can you come into the report room?"

Melanie could see Charlie standing a few feet behind him, and figured they were up to something. She left her area reluctantly and walked to the small room used by officers to write reports. The two guys followed her into the empty room, and the look on Ted's face told her this was no joke.

"They told us in roll call that a guy washed up on Cabrillo Beach today. He'd been stabbed—And Mel, they ID'd him as—Enzo Mancini."

The blood drained from her face, and her legs wobbled. Ted reached for her and caught her before she hit the ground. He pulled her to him, and she buried her face in his shoulder, but her sobs could still be heard through-out the halls of the station.

"I'm sorry, Mel," Ted said. "But I didn't know how else to tell you."

1997

Shaking off her memories, Melanie said, "We were, uh, seeing each other, and—"

"Mama always suspected another woman," Adriana interrupted.

Scott stiffened. "Why haven't I heard of this guy?"

"There wasn't any reason to bring it up. He'd promised to meet me one night, but he never showed up. All of a sudden it struck her that she was talking to Enzo's flesh and blood, and she touched the girl's face as she said, "Then a few days later his body washed up on the shore."

Adriana grabbed Scott's arm. "He drowned?"

"The coroner said he'd been stabbed to death."

Scott's eyes widened. "Jesus, by who?"

"They never found out. They assumed it was a drug thing."

"And what did you think?" Scott glared at his mother.

"I didn't want to believe it, but there was so much I didn't know about him."

Scott's voiced quivered. "And yet you were sleeping with him?"

"I was twenty-one, Scott, and in love."

Adriana broke her silence. "He didn't tell you about my mother?"

"He told me that six months before we met, he and your mother fought about her coming to America. That she wouldn't do it, and he felt their relationship was over. If he knew about a pregnancy, he didn't mention it to me."

Scott had heard enough and walked away, standing with his back to both women.

"Does Dad know?"

"Of course. He was living here at the time, and he was a great help to me afterward. But we've never talked about it since."

Scott left to take Adriana home, and Melanie walked to the bar and poured herself a drink. She took it to a booth and sat in the dim light of the neon beer signs scattered around the room. What just happened? Enzo Mancini, a name that she had tucked away in the recesses of her mind was back to remind her how losing him that way had altered the course of her life.

CHAPTER 5

1973

HARBOR DETECTIVES HAD worked for a month with the Port of Los Angeles Police Department to find Enzo's killer. They interviewed his crew members, friends, other boat owners, their crew members, and sailors. They found no eyewitnesses to the events of the night of the murder, nor any motives other than evidence of dope smuggling. Everyone said he had been a quiet guy, who kept to himself when in port. The crime went unsolved.

Melanie had taken almost two weeks off after Enzo's death. During that time. she hadn't spoken to Benny any more than necessary. Every time she looked at him, her stomach tightened, and she wished she could afford to move into her own place.

Benny tried to make small talk, but Melanie wouldn't thaw. "Where have you been? I miss your singing."

Melanie shuffled through some sheet music in a drawer. "I found some good-paying singing gigs in Torrance and Wilmington."

"Guess I should up my pay so I can see more of you," Benny said with a smile.

She bit her bottom lip to refrain from saying what she felt.

He cleared his throat. "The boys at the PD had any luck finding Mancini's killer?"

Melanie slammed the drawer shut. "Why do you care? You're glad he's dead!"

"I can't deny that I'm happy he's gone. He was no good for you. You deserve better."

"Well, you got what you wanted, didn't you?" she said under her breath as she walked out the back door.

After returning to work at Harbor Station, she continued to perform for local clubs. But she still needed another diversion to take her mind off Enzo and Benny. She volunteered her time to help the Harbor Division female Community Relations Officer with the girls' Explorer Scout Program. It kept her busy, and she enjoyed working with them on community projects.

Meanwhile, Ted took her out for meals, movies, and ball games. It helped her save money to move, and he became a refuge from her grief and a buffer between her and her father. Before she knew it, three months had passed since Enzo's death, and though she still felt the sting of that awful night, at least the gnawing in her gut had finally subsided.

MELANIE AND TED decided to go a steakhouse for dinner on a night off work. When they arrived home at McNeil's, Ted turned to go into his room inside the bar, and Melanie stood at the foot of the stairway to her studio apartment.

"I rented a couple of videos today. Why don't you come up?"

He smiled. "I hope they're not more women's lib stories."

She threw her shoulders back. "Actually one is a "cop story."

Ted followed her upstairs and made himself comfortable on the convertible couch that doubled as Melanie's bed. The videotapes were on the coffee table, so he picked one up and slid it into the VCR. While the tape cued up, Melanie went to her compact kitchen.

"Want a beer?" she asked.

"Don't I always?"

"Come to think of it, yes."

She grabbed a couple of bottles from the refrigerator and sat down next to him in front of the TV.

As usual, his arm was draped around her shoulders throughout most of the movie. She had come to feel secure with it there. She felt the same way about how he often placed his hand in the small of her back when they stood in lines and such. Since he never attempted to take things further, she appreciated those simple but comforting gestures.

The second movie wasn't as good as the reviews had said, and halfway through it she fell asleep in the crook of Ted's arm. She awoke as the credits rolled and gazed up at him.

He smiled down at her. "Hey, sleepyhead," he said, but didn't move a muscle.

She rubbed her face on his chest and realized it was time to get up, but she didn't want to leave the cocoon he had formed around her. Instead, she clung to him tighter. He brushed his mouth over her forehead, pushing her hair out of her eyes.

Half asleep, her next move was instinctive. She lifted her face toward his and caught his lips with hers. He reciprocated by wrapping his other arm around her and deepening the kiss. To her surprise, it warmed her all over, and she didn't want it to end.

He must've recognized that, because he eased her back on the couch and began caressing her face and neck. Without a second thought, she unbuttoned her blouse.

"You're beautiful," Ted said as he explored her breasts, and soon they had both shed their clothing and lay fondling each other.

There had been no man in her bed before or since Enzo. She had fallen in love with Enzo because he was different from other guys she'd met at the bar and police station. He was shy and introspective, and she trusted him. By the time they had gone to bed together, she had seen the "wanting her" look in his eyes, and when they made love his hunger fueled hers, too.

That night, Melanie saw much of that desire in Ted's face as he moved atop her. Despite not feeling the sense of urgency she had had with Enzo, the pleasure she gave Ted aroused her, and she was delighted to reach an explosive climax of her own.

———

THE NIGHT OF passion with Ted had been a turning point in Melanie's grief. It made her realize what she'd had with Enzo might've been merely an exciting physical attraction intensified by periods of separation and sexual tension. However, she still mourned the man she'd known and couldn't get beyond her father's obvious satisfaction with Enzo's death.

As she feared, Ted interpreted their encounter as the beginning of a love affair.

"Hey, I picked up a movie for us tonight. We can dine in and relax afterward like we did last week." Ted winked. "What d'ya say?"

"Oh, sorry," she said. "I can't. I have a gig at a restaurant in Long Beach. A guy who works there said he could arrange for me to meet his friend who has a recording studio."

"I don't like you going off to meet strange guys by yourself."

"I'm taking Karen with me. I'll be fine."

MELANIE WAS SCHEDULED to record the demo tape in three weeks. While she waited, President Richard Nixon's reputation worsened with every revelation that surfaced during the Watergate hearings. To add to the dysfunction in the country, the Vietnam War still raged on, despite the growing anti-war sentiment on the home front.

She had a chance to learn more about the effects of the war when she accepted a date with an old boyfriend who had recently been discharged from the Army. They had dated a few times in high school, but because he didn't have a college deferment he was drafted right after graduation in 1969.

It was good to see Hank. He still had his loveable crooked smile, but he had matured in both body and spirit. She was sure he'd grown a couple of inches, and he'd developed the brawn and stature of the man in the cigarette ads. He had, in fact, turned into a hunk.

But the light in his eyes had faded, and his sun-parched face was drawn, appearing to reflect the pain and horrors he had seen in the jungles on the other side of the world. Somehow the angst she had suffered in her own life during the same time period seemed trivial. She made up her mind then to live each day to its fullest, and try to make the best of everything that came her way.

THE RECORDING SESSION day finally arrived. After being introduced to the technician, she had spent the next two weeks rehearsing and recording. She could barely remember a time when she hadn't hoped and prayed for this day. Melanie drove away from the studio with her demo tape next to her on the seat. She glanced over at it every few minutes, as she drove, to assure herself she hadn't dreamed the whole thing.

Of course, this marked only the beginning. Now the really hard work began: finding an agent. She had received the names of a few of them from the singers and musicians she'd work with, but the issue of meeting them still remained. And would one of them like her music well enough to represent her?

She told everyone she knew, "I mailed a copy of my tape to all of the agents on my list, and now I wait."

Of everyone, Benny was the happiest. He had encouraged her singing from the time he'd first heard her sing in church. Until a short time ago, she had wanted to succeed the most for him. Ironically, with the state of their relationship, now she resented his enthusiasm.

It had been over a month since Melanie sent out her demo tapes and she began to get discouraged.

"So, have you heard from those agents you contacted?" Caroline asked her for the third time in two weeks.

"Nope. Still waiting," She answered each time.

It was disappointing not to hear from at least one agent, but even harder to have to keep telling people she hadn't.

It helped that her busy schedule with work, singing, and the Explorers, kept her from dwelling on her disappointment.

"Hey Mel, how about going to an early movie tonight before work?" Ted asked. It sounded harmless enough. There wouldn't be time for a repeat performance in her bed like the last time.

ANOTHER TWO WEEKS passed with no response from an agent. She did however receive a call from her doctor's office.

"The test results are in, Miss McNeil. You're pregnant."

Melanie's insides turned to ice, and she couldn't breathe, let alone speak.

"Are you there, Miss McNeil?"

"Uh, yes."

"Doctor will want to see you in two weeks. Please call the front desk for an appointment as soon as possible."

Melanie hadn't heard exactly what the nurse said, but she croaked out, "Okay. Thank you."

Once reality sank in, she considered terminating the pregnancy. With Roe v. Wade having passed only a few months earlier, abortion was in the forefront of the news and of her mind. But having been raised by an Irish Catholic father and Portuguese Catholic mother, she couldn't bring herself to do it. Adoption could be the solution, she thought. She had known girls in high school who had given their babies to adoption agencies.

Of course, she could keep the child, but it seemed almost impossible without her father's financial help. She knew if she stayed with him she had to finally face her suspicions head on. Her father had no alibi for the night of Enzo's death, and she had witnessed his capacity for violence first hand. There was no way she would bring her child up under his roof. Melanie would have some time to choose, but the fact remained, whatever her decision, she owed it to Ted to talk to him about it.

Ted's face glowed, as he listened to Melanie's news later on in her room. He grabbed her by the shoulders and planted a smacking kiss on her mouth. "This is wonderful. When?"

"Next spring. But we need to make some decisions soon."

"Of course." He sat on the couch. "Like when and where the ceremony will be."

"But Ted, I'm not sure I want to get married."

"What?"

"There are other alternatives, you know."

He tensed up. "Abortion?"

"No, but we could consider adoption."

His eyes dropped. "You want to give our child to strangers?"

"It would be a way to move forward with our plans after the pregnancy."

"But we could do it as a family."

"That might work for you. You'll continue to do police work. Your career won't miss a beat. But what about mine? My dream?"

Ted took her hands in his. "We can make that work, too."

Melanie tried hard to choose her words with care. "Ted, I care a lot for you. You've been my rock after Enzo died, but I can't say I'm in love with you."

He wrapped his arms around her. "I love you enough for both us. And our love for the baby will bring us closer than ever."

Ted's profession of love and the reassurance she could continue her own career wooed her into marrying him. But the prospect of having a permanent sanctuary away from Benny was what clinched the deal.

THEIR WEDDING TOOK place on a chilly day in November at the "Wayfarers Chapel," an historic glass church on the cliffs above Palos Verdes. Melanie would've been happy with a weekend wedding in Las Vegas, but Ted was able to book the church during the off-season for a reasonable price. Despite the small and simple affair, he wanted to have a "real" wedding with the bride and groom in traditional garb. Most attendees were friends from the police department and McNeil's Pub, where the reception took place.

The newlyweds moved into a small apartment in neighboring

Torrance. Soon after, Ted was promoted to a training officer and transferred to night watch, working patrol from four to midnight. Her morning watch shift, from midnight to eight, made it difficult for them to be together. They found themselves exchanging quick kisses in the property room on their way in and out of the station.

"Hey Mel, I miss ya," Ted said after one particularly hectic week. "How about cutting back on the singing jobs for a while?"

"Ted, it won't be long before I'm too big to perform. I need to do it as long as I can."

"Well I'd like to meet my wife in our bed occasionally instead of this room."

BY THE END of February 1974, Melanie had to stop booking singing gigs. She did continue working at the station, but switched to night watch to be on the same schedule as Ted. That pleased him, but the reality was even though his patrol hours were four to midnight, he had to testify in court in downtown LA at 8:00 a.m. on an average of three times a week. So, with the exception of the weekends, they were back to meeting in the property room. One of those times he had news.

"Mel, my promotion to senior lead officer finally came through. I showed up on the transfer list to Newton Division, and I report at the beginning of the next deployment period."

"Oh that will work out good, since I start my pregnancy leave next month. The loss of my paycheck won't hurt our bank account as much."

Ted worked night watch at Newton Division, located northeast of San Pedro in south-central LA. Gangs ran rampant in this area and made up the majority of Ted's arrests. His phone calls at end of watch to Melanie became more frequent as time went on.

"Hey honey, how are you and the baby doing?"

"We're okay. How late do you expect to be tonight?"

"We just booked a couple of women for dope, but we have to transport them to Sybil Brand Jail. So, I'll be pretty late. Don't wait up."

"Oh, I won't," Melanie said. She tried to believe him, but she'd overheard that line from officers talking to their wives at Harbor Station many times, when she knew they were end of watch and off to a bar with their buddies.

Ted said, "See you in the morning. Love you."

Melanie hung up the phone, studied the small apartment and shook her head. How did I end up here? She asked herself. I was on my way to the career of my dreams. Instead I sit here alone with Ted's child in my belly.

WITH TED AWAY so much of the time, and with no word from a music agent, Melanie reached out more to her friend, Karen. She stopped by a club one night to watch Karen perform with the old band. It was great seeing everyone, but she soon found herself wishing she was on the stage.

So she invited the gang over to her place. She wanted her friends to meet Ted. He was end of watch at midnight, and with any luck he wouldn't have to work overtime.

She left the club for home, by way of the liquor store, to pick up beer and snacks. When she got home, she straightened up the apartment, put out the food, and waited for Ted and her guests. Ted called about eleven to tell her he should be getting off about midnight, but Karen and the guys showed up around 11:30. A couple of the guys brought dates, and Karen's boyfriend arrived a few minutes later. By then, the small apartment was wall-to-wall people.

"So this is what marital bliss looks like," Josh remarked as he glanced around the apartment.

"This is it," Melanie stretched out her arms. "It's not so bad."

"Don't you miss performing?"

"I do miss the singing," she said with a smile. "and the applause."

"Well, if it makes you feel any better, people ask about you all of the time," Karen said.

"It does."

"Hey," Larry said, jumping up. "You've got an audience right here." He reached for the guitar he'd brought with him. "Come on Mel, let's jam." He strummed a few chords. "This is one of your best."

"Oh, I don't know. The neighbors won't like it."

The others chimed in and egged her on. Melanie couldn't resist. She took a breath and eased into the song.

After two songs, Ted walked into his living room and looked around until he spotted Melanie, deep in conversation with one of her female guests. He wound through the crowd toward his wife.

Melanie sat up at the sight of him and glanced at the clock on the wall. "Oh, Ted. It's about time. Get something to drink, and join us."

He went to the refrigerator and snatched a can of beer. Before he could pull the tab off the can, Melanie walked up to him and kissed him on the cheek.

"You said you'd be here earlier."

"Something came up."

"It always does," she said under her breath. How many times had she heard that? Grabbing his hand, she led him across the room. "Come on, I want to introduce you to some friends."

Melanie called for their attention and presented Ted to the group.

One of the guys joked, "Watch out, the fuzz is here now."

Ted smiled and simulated drawing a gun from an invisible holster at his side. Everyone got a good laugh, and went back to what they were doing. Melanie tried to bring Ted into the conversation as he sipped his beer. But he appeared bored and only chatted a few minutes with Karen and her boyfriend then announced he was going to bed.

Melanie followed him into the bedroom. "That was rude of you. We waited all that time for you to get here, and then you say two words and go to bed."

"I'm beat."

"How many times have you gone out with the guys after work? You say it helps you wind down."

"It does."

"Then why can't you do that with my friends?"

"It's not the same."

"But I wanted you to get to know them."

"I met 'em. They seem okay. Now go back in there and enjoy yourself. I'm going to bed."

This was not the first time this kind of thing had happened. Whenever she tried to mix her civilian friends with Ted, he withdrew. As familiar as she thought she was with cops, she'd never realized this was not uncommon among them.

The longer she and Ted were married the more she had come to realize the bravado that he and his fellow officers exhibited was driven by a distrust of civilians. As first responders they saw people at their worst and were repeatedly forced to deal with the carnage that people often inflicted upon each other. All too often they found themselves in the middle of family disputes that reversed on a dime when both parties decided to take their frustrations out on the officer. And after encountering enough people whose resistance often led to life-threatening physical confrontations, they became skittish in the presence of people they didn't know and trust.

This "us against them" attitude was hard for Melanie to come to terms with. She was still learning when to challenge it and when to let it go. This night she decided not to let it interfere with enjoying the company of her friends.

———

THE FIRST TIME she felt the baby kicking, it took her by surprise and she experienced a kind of love she never had before. Until then, the only thing that had elicited a similar feeling was singing. By then she was ready for her leave from work, to prepare for the baby, due in mid-May.

On a Friday a couple of weeks later, Melanie waddled into her apartment out of breath, carrying a couple of grocery bags and the mail. She dropped them on the kitchen counter and eased into the nearest chair. The baby was due at any time, and the smallest amount of physical exercise wore her out.

She had heard it would be like this, but always having a trim figure, she couldn't really imagine it. It was bad enough she couldn't sleep at night because of heartburn and numerous trips to the bathroom, but this was ridiculous. Despite the fact that some maternal instincts had recently kicked in, she vowed to forever use birth control after the baby was born.

After peeing and putting the groceries away, she plopped on the couch, turned the TV on, and flipped the channel to a news station.

She sorted through the mail: mostly bills. Without looking up at the screen, she assumed the sound of gunfire she heard came from coverage of the never-ending war zones of Vietnam. She switched to another channel then froze as she glimpsed several men in familiar blue uniforms gripping shotguns, while crouched behind cars, walls, and other barriers.

She watched them duck bullets and explosions as the commentator announced that the SLA or Symbionese Liberation Army, a group responsible for the kidnapping of Patricia Hearst, the daughter of publisher William Randolph Hearst, were holed up in a house in south central LA., and were attempting to hold LAPD officers at bay with automatic weapons.

"Holy Jeeze!"

When she learned it was taking place in Newton division she began to pace around the room. And when she heard that hundreds of officers were at the scene, a wave of nausea swept over her, and she swooned a bit.

"Oh my God," she whispered. "Ted must be there." She dropped onto the couch.

She sat with eyes glued to the screen, searching for Ted, to no avail. The SLA members were relentless in their effort to "kill the fascist pigs;" their battle cry for the past two months.

Gunshots continued for over an hour, as Melanie agonized over Ted's fate. She sat facing the fears that had kept her from dating policemen. "What if he is injured, or killed? What about the baby? I can't raise it alone."

Her thoughts turned to the pressure she felt in her womb. Pressure that soon became sharp pains.

"Oh dear. Not now! Not without Ted!" she said out loud and phoned Caroline.

Soon there was a knock at the door. "Oh, thank God you're here." Melanie said to Caroline, as she let her in the apartment.

"How far apart are the contractions?"

"About ten minutes."

"Okay. Try to relax." Caroline glanced over at the TV. "That's not helping. Did you call the station?"

"No."

"I'll call and ask for Ted. From what I hear, SWAT is handling it."

"I know, but everybody around there is in danger." Melanie said as her pains increased and began to last longer.

Caroline hung up the phone. "There have been no officers injured. They'll tell Ted about the contractions as soon as possible. Is your bag packed and ready to go?"

"Yes," Melanie said.

"Good. I grabbed a deck of cards before I left." She turned off the TV and started to deal the cards. "And I play a mean game of Gin Rummy."

Melanie had never been so glad to see Ted as when he entered the delivery room. Deep in labor by then, her eyes filled with tears as he took her hand and kissed it. Within an hour she was writhing in pain and cursing him.

Finally, the doctor exclaimed, "It's a boy."

CHAPTER 6

1997

AFTER HEARING MELANIE'S story about Enzo's death, Scott and Adriana entered her motel room in a seedy neighborhood of San Pedro. Adriana flipped a wall switch, and the overhead light came on.

"Well, this it." She threw her purse on one of the queen size beds and went into the bathroom.

Scott cringed at the sight of the place. He didn't know what to say and took a seat on the edge of a torn stuffed chair.

"You know," Adriana called from the toilet, "It's because of your mother that I never knew my father."

"That's not fair. She thought it was over with your mother."

Adriana came out and sat on the bed. "You don't know how hard it was for Mama when he didn't come back. She was a woman shamed."

Scott winced and shifted in his chair.

"How was she supposed to support us alone?"

"She didn't have a family to help?" Scott asked.

"They threw her out of the house. So she married that swine, Theo, and he took her back to Greece with him."

"So that's why your name is Dimakos," Scott murmured.

"He was, what you call here? A cheapskate. And when she died, he put me out on the street!" Adriana teared up. "My only hope was to find my father. I've always dreamed he lived here in wealth, and he would take me in."

"I'm sorry," Scott said.

"And instead, I'm forced to live like this."

"Adriana, I can't change what happened, but I promise you I'll make it better somehow."

"You would do that for me?"

"Of course. And I know my mother will help, too. Now I'd better go, so you can get some rest." He kissed her forehead. "I'll call you tomorrow."

"But, I'm afraid of Marco."

"What did you promise him for helping you find your father?"

"A few dollars. Not as much as he's trying to get from me."

Scott shook his head and contemplated his options. "I can bunk out on the other bed."

"Oh, thank you so much," Adriana said, then stepped back into the bathroom.

As the shower ran in the background, Scott took off his shoes and unbuckled his belt. He stretched out on the bed, turned the TV on, and flipped through the channels. He began to envision her standing there; water running down her cleavage, and realized this may not have been a good idea after all. This could be a really long night with her in touching distance, and me trying to behave better than that lowlife, Marco.

He removed his pants, slid under the covers and turned over. He closed his eyes, hoping to erase her image from his mind, and subdue his hard-on. Neither one diminished. His only hope was sleep, so he tried to relax.

Once finished with her shower, Adriana slipped into the other side of his bed and whispered in his ear, "Are you awake?

He turned over and found her mouth with his. From there she led the way. Lifting her gown, she climbed on top of him and rocked slowly over his damp briefs until he yanked the front of them down to allow her to take him inside.

When both were spent, she placed her head on his chest. "I've got to find out about my father."

Scott gasped for air. "What?"

"Who killed him."

"But that was twenty-four years ago."

"I came to this country to find him. Please, I have to know!"

Scott lifted her face up from his chest, and kissed her softly.

The next day, Scott helped Adriana pack up her things, and he moved her to his apartment. He told her he couldn't leave her in that rat hole, but more than that, he wanted her in his bed every night. She gave him no argument, and wasted no time settling into his place.

HE WENT TO work on a high the next day, and anxious to talk to Charlie about looking into Mancini's murder.

"Jesus, I never thought I'd hear about that goddamned Italian again. And your mother told you about her relationship with him? Kinda funny that now you're screwing his daughter."

Scott ignored his wisecrack and played with some pens in a cup on Charlie's desk. "It's more than that."

"Yeah, sure. True love."

"Well, yeah."

Charlie shook his head and rolled his eyes. "Shit."

"I'm only asking you to take a look at the case. See if there've been any follow-ups done."

"Hell, I'll bet nobody's touched it in years."

"Doesn't somebody pull those cold cases out once in a while?" Scott said.

"Nobody gives a shit about a foreign sailor whacked by one of his dope connections."

"My mother did."

"Maybe, but not anymore. Now she's married to an assistant chief who's about to become chief."

"Mom said his shipmate ran off before the detectives could talk to him."

Charlie shrugged. "So run a check on him."

"I really could use your help."

"Why don't you ask your old man?"

"He's up to his ass in politics."

"And I'm very happy with my caseload just the way it is." Charlie stood up. "I do enough to get by. That's all I want to do till I pull the pin. Now, let's go. I've got to see a guy about a set of golf clubs."

———

ADRIANA DROVE UP to Melanie's house in a candy apple red sports car. Scott jumped out of the passenger seat. "Wait here, I'll see if Mom's home."

A few minutes later, Melanie trailed Scott to the car. She leaned over and peeked inside. "Hi, Adriana. Nice car."

"She needed a car, so we went shopping yesterday," Scott said.

"Isn't it beautiful?" Adriana got out of the car. "The traffic driving here was awful. Can I use your bathroom?"

"Of course. It's the second door to your left from the entryway."

Melanie stood back for a better look at the car. "First your apartment, now this?"

"Yup." he answered. "What do you think of it?"

"It's beautiful, honey, but are you sure you can afford it?"

"Sure. What else have I got to spend my money on?"

Melanie ignored the question and climbed into the driver's seat.

Scott leaned into the window and tried to win her over. "I knew you'd like it. It's your style."

She toyed with the knobs on the dash. "What's not to like? It fits her perfectly: foreign, expensive, and dangerous."

"You forgot to mention gorgeous."

"Which makes all the rest totally unimportant, doesn't it?"

"Mom, there's more to her than that. You don't know her."

Melanie turned to him. "Scott, I know her better than you can imagine."

———

IT WAS LATE in the day, and Charlie sat nursing a drink and conversing with the bartender in the Bronze Anchor, a small police hangout. The bartender nodded to Charlie and cocked is head toward Melanie as she walked in wearing fitted pants and a top to match, her hair caressing her shoulders.

"Hey, that your partner's mother?"

"Holy shit. Yeah."

He made his way toward her.

She appeared to recognize him, but squinted to see beyond his gray hair and crow's feet. "Charlie?"

"Sure."

She stepped closer to him and held out her hand. "How are you?"

"Pretty much the way I look. And you must be terrific."

Her body relaxed and her mouth turned up. "I was afraid you wouldn't recognize me."

"Never happen."

"Scott's been talking about you so much I—"

"I think I embarrassed him a little. Don't think he ever heard his mother described quite that way before."

Melanie blushed. "So that's why he looked at me so funny the day he told me about you."

"He's a good kid. Sharp, too. Just a little too gung ho for this burned-out copper."

She waved his comment off. "I don't believe that."

He motioned for her to sit across from him in the booth.

"Ted's still going strong, though. Won't be long before you'll be the wife of the chief of police."

"We'll see," Melanie said, but changed the subject to the reason for her visit. "Charlie, I came here to ask you a favor."

"This have anything to do with the Mancini case?"

"How did you know?"

"Christ, Mel. I can't believe Scott sent you. I told him to leave it alone. He's just hot for the broad. It'll pass."

"I know that. It's why I don't want you to help him."

Charlie answered with surprise. "You don't?"

"I thought for sure it was your kind of case."

He shrugged. "Once upon a time."

"And here I was prepared to rant and rave, bargain and plead— whatever it would take—Maybe even flirt a little."

"Damn. I'd have loved to see that."

Melanie turned her face away from him. "Me too. I'm not very good at it."

"You never had to be. All you had to do was walk into a room."

"That was a long time ago."

Charlie grinned. "Oh, I don' know. This joint hasn't been the same since you showed up."

Melanie felt herself starting to buy his line and changed the subject. "So what have you been doing all these years?"

"Thinking about you," he said with that familiar flirty smile.

Melanie giggled and shook her head.

"Still dodging my passes, I see."

"Habit, I guess."

He turned serious. "I figured you'd want to reopen the case. If not for the girl, for yourself."

"It won't bring him back, only a lot of bad memories. Besides, I don't trust her."

"Well, I won't open it officially, but I can't stop Scott from checking into it on his own."

"Will you let me know what he's doing?"

"Sure. Here's my card," he said and jotted a number on it. "I put my home phone on the back. You'd better call me there instead of the office."

She took it, and he asked, "Have you got a business card?"

She pulled one out of her purse and handed it to him. "Call me on my mobile number. Thanks, Charlie. I'm sorry you got dragged into this."

He stared into her eyes. "I was too, until a few minutes ago."

———

CHARLIE RECEIVED A call from Ted early the next morning to meet at a coffee shop in Wilmington, located at the north end of

Harbor division. They ordered breakfast and reminisced about their glory days as they ate.

Midway through the meal, Ted changed the subject. "Well, I didn't really ask you to meet me here to talk about old times."

"I figured that," Charlie said.

"I'm concerned about Scott and the Mancini case."

"He's a pretty determined kid."

"I know, but I'm afraid he's going to start kicking up more shit than Melanie needs," Ted said.

"I tried to talk him out of it but—"

"She's pretty vulnerable right now, because of her father's death. I thought running the bar was a bad idea, but to make matters worse, the girl shows up and dredges up more of the past. I don't know how much of this she can take."

"If I remember, she's a pretty tough cookie."

"I know my wife!"

Charlie tensed up. "Look, I feel like I'm in the middle of a family dispute. First Scott begs me to open the case. Then Melanie asks me not to, and now I get the feeling I'm about to be ordered to leave it alone."

"Melanie asked you not to get involved?"

"Hell, yeah." Charlie shook his head. "Jesus, I'm only a salty detective with two busted marriages, but I can see you people need to talk to each other more."

"You just keep Scott away from the case."

"Listen, I'll do what I can," Charlie said. "But he's trying to be the girl's hero so he can stay in her panties. Even as his senior officer I can't compete with that."

CHAPTER 7

1998 ARRIVED WITH the usual amount of New Year fanfare, and once again Melanie found herself doing her duty as the supportive wife of the assistant chief. Ted's purview stretched from the northern San Fernando Valley, to the southern tip of the city of LA. This time the function was a chamber of commerce mixer in the San Pedro area, in a restaurant high on the cliffs overlooking the ocean.

Melanie tried to circulate, but made her way to a familiar face. She and Alice Morton had worked together on a couple of civic projects and had hit off. So much so that, she shared her plans about the nightclub with her.

"So what are you going to call it?"

"McNeil's, of course."

Melanie saw Ted waving her over with a drink in his hand, and Alice saw it, too. "What's Ted think of the idea?"

Melanie winked at her and smiled, then turned toward Ted. "I'll let you know when I tell him."

She caught Ted's eye as she approached him where he stood with two other men.

"Hello, Martin," she said. "How are you?"

"It's always good to see you, Melanie."

She extended her hand to the other fellow. "I'm afraid we haven't met. I'm Melanie Swain."

"I'm Jack. Nice to meet you. Ted was telling us how much time you've put in at the Watts Children Center lately."

"I've enjoyed it."

"I'm sorry to hear about your father," Martin said.

"Thank you."

"And you've kept his bar open?"

"Yes, and I'm planning to remodel it, and open a nightclub."

Out of the corner of her eye, she saw Ted's mouth drop open. Then he took a gulp of his drink.

The man's face lit up. "I like it. It could really stimulate some much-needed business in this town."

Melanie smiled. "I hope so."

"Ted, you never mentioned anything about this," Martin said.

"Hey, it may also be a good excuse for our chief to spend more time in our neck of the woods," Jack added.

Ted downed his drink and set it on a table. "Well, we're not sure about this."

Melanie shot him a dirty look, but he continued, "Look, fellas, it was good talking to you, but I promised Jeff Michaels we'd discuss some security issues at his plant."

He directed her away and toward the bar. "Bourbon and soda," he said to the bartender.

While waiting, he leaned over and whispered to her, "What the hell was all that bullshit?"

"It wasn't bullshit. I'm really planning on doing it."

"And this is how you tell me?"

"If you'd been home for more than ten minutes this past month, I might've been able to tell you sooner."

He grabbed his glass off the bar and took a long drink. "Well, I know now, and I hate the idea! Now go mingle. That's why you're here."

She wanted to lash out at him, but remembered her place and went into the ladies' room to compose herself. When she came out, two guys she had never met approached her. They introduced themselves as Bart and Alex, and she proceeded to make small talk with them.

At one point in the conversation, Bart managed to ease his hand around her waist and place it on her lower back. She tried to step away from him, but he stayed with her. She was about to remove his hand when Ted walked up and yanked Bart's hand off of her.

"That's off limits, guy."

Melanie spun around and saw the anger on Ted's face, so she chuckled. "Oh, oh," she said. "He caught us."

Bart smiled. "Hey Ted, sorry about that. You've got a pretty engaging lady here."

"That doesn't give you the right to— Melanie took Ted's arm, and said, "Bart was just telling me he's a former San Francisco detective."

"I know." Ted said.

"Sure. Ted and I go way back."

Ted mumbled. "Yeah, once an asshole, always an asshole."

Melanie knew she had to get Ted out of there. "Uh, please excuse us. Good to meet you both."

She took Ted's arm and led him toward the exit. "What's the matter with you?"

"With me? You're the one hanging on that guy."

She spoke out of the side of her mouth, so as not to be heard by the others as they walked toward the door. "You think I enjoy that?"

He didn't answer.

"Well, I don't, but I would've handled it without making a scene.

You tell me to mingle and then you walk up and practically throw a choke hold on the guy."

As they walked across the parking lot to their car Melanie noticed Ted staggering. "How many drinks did you have tonight?" she asked.

"Not enough."

Once in the car, Ted burned rubber out of the lot, and Melanie asked, "What's wrong? I've never seen you drink so much at one of these things?"

"Leave me alone."

"Why are you so against my plan?"

"Because you're my wife, not some fucking saloon owner."

"Ted, please slow down. In fact, let me drive."

He ignored her and continued to speed, veering in and out of his lane into oncoming traffic.

"A nightclub can be a very respectable business."

"Respectable, my ass. Surrounded by a bunch of lowlife guys, looking to get laid every night. I thought we agreed you wouldn't work right now."

She knew it was futile to argue with him in his drunken state. "Let's talk about this later, Ted."

He ignored her suggestion. "Didn't we agree?"

"But it's been almost a year. I need to do something."

"So my career is not important to you anymore?"

She knew him. He wasn't going to let this go. "I didn't say that, but I should've taken that promotion instead of becoming a trophy on your arm."

She watched him take a wrong turn leading them higher up the curvy San Pedro hills. "Ted, where are you going?"

He stepped harder on the gas and nearly rammed into the rear end of a car stopped at a stop sign. The force of it made her brace herself on the dashboard.

"Damn it, Ted. Let me drive!"

"So being my wife is not enough for you anymore?"

She grabbed the strap above her head and used the other hand to grip the dash. She had to get him to stop the car. "I don't even know if I can get permits for the re-model. It may not even work out after all."

"Melanie, why the fuck did you marry me? You never even noticed me until Mancini bought it."

He turned to her and started to grab her, just as someone stepped off the curb at an intersection. "Mel, listen to me…"

Melanie saw the pedestrian just about to cross their path and yelled, "Look out!"

Ted twisted the steering wheel with both hands, spinning the car 180 degrees and missing the pedestrian by inches. "Shit."

Melanie took a deep breath, jumped out of the car, and spoke to him through the open door. She pointed to the convenience store on the corner. "Come on. Let's go in the store. You can get some coffee, and I'll drive us home."

He sat there motionless, staring straight ahead.

"Well, I'm not getting back in this car with you! I'll call a cab if I have to." She slammed the door and waited to see if he would get out, but instead he stepped on the gas and left her standing on the road.

Melanie watched his taillights fade from sight. Goddamn him.

She paced around where she stood for a few minutes, reliving the past couple of hours. Maybe she shouldn't have told him about her plans the way she did, although it had worked at the restaurant when she told him she wanted to keep the bar. What provoked such a violent response from him this time?

When people started noticing her standing there, she reached for her phone in her purse and called Scott. She heard his answering machine and headed for the store. She slipped her phone back into its place and noticed the business card Charlie had given her. She knew he lived nearby. Why not? *I need to talk to somebody.*

CHARLIE SHOWED UP within a half an hour in his SUV, and at her request, he parked in the lot near a deserted area of the beach. She wasn't ready to face Ted at home, and had missed walking on the beach at night since living in the Valley. She jumped out of the truck and took off toward the water, kicking her shoes off along the way. With Charlie right behind her, she reached the tide line, stopped, and took deep breath.

"He'd been drinking more than usual tonight," she said. "But I wasn't ready for him to go ballistic." She began to walk. "I really thought he was going to hit that guy."

Charlie followed along. "Sounds like the Ted Swain I know."

"But he never loses his cool anymore. I can't remember the last time we fought."

"Bad day at the office?"

"I didn't think so."

"I wouldn't worry too much about it."

"Maybe it's the stress catching up to him," she said.

"And what about you? How are you holding up?"

"Oh, I'm fine. Or at least I was until tonight."

Charlie grabbed her arm, and they stopped walking. "Your husband's about to become the top cop of LAPD, you've just decided to close one business and open another, and your dead lover's daughter shows up to seduce your son into resurrecting a lot of old wounds. Call me a chauvinistic bastard, but I think it's a lot for one woman to deal with."

Melanie giggled. "You, a chauvinist?

"Talk to my last wife. She was an expert on that shit."

Melanie laughed, took the pins out of her wind-blown hair, and let it fall onto her shoulders.

"That's the way I like it," Charlie said.

Melanie pretended to ignore the remark. "How are your kids, Charlie?"

"The oldest just graduated from San Diego State. She's getting married in a few months." He sighed. The youngest just finished rehab and blames me for her addiction."

She touched his arm. "I'm sorry."

"Oh, hell, she's probably right. When her mother told me to leave, I was a real asshole about it. I hardly ever saw the kids."

"The job has killed more than a few marriages."

"It's a good excuse, anyway." Charlie turned and faced the water. "You know, I was surprised you'd married Ted so soon after Mancini."

She sat down and wiggled her toes in the sand. "Well, I, uh, got pregnant with Ted's baby and—"

"Whoa," Charlie said with a shit-eating grin. "How'd that happen?"

She stuck her tongue out at him, "—and he asked me to marry him. I didn't want an abortion, and I didn't have many choices. I couldn't stay with my father after Enzo's murder."

He joined her on the sand. "And what about now?"

"Now, I can't imagine my life without Scott."

"So your marriage amounts to nothing more than one roll in the hay twenty-five years ago? Doesn't say much for Ted."

"Look, you're talking to the woman he dumped on the highway. You expect me to throw him roses?"

"Not me. He's the guy who caught the woman I was chasing. You can throw him to the goddamn press as far as I'm concerned."

"Wouldn't they love this story?"

"You that mad?"

Melanie nodded. "But I've managed to keep the media at bay so far, and I don't intend to make us both look ridiculous."

"I'm surprised he's never jumped in your shit like this before. It's his MO."

"I've never crossed him before. Not about something so important."

"Not even your singing career?"

She smiled. "You remember that?"

"Sure. For the longest time I kept expecting to hear you pop up on the radio. Did you ever make that tape?"

Melanie nodded. "Yes. I was looking for an agent when I found out about the baby."

The sound of the waves crashing onto the shore filled the dead space between them. Then Charlie asked, "What if he doesn't budge on the club?"

"I'm not going to let him stop me."

"Good for you."

"Because seeing you again reminds me of how I felt before Ted; like I could do anything."

He bent his head toward her face, and when she didn't turn away, he kissed her tenderly on the lips. With his next kiss, she put her arms around him and kissed him harder.

Taking her cue, he pushed her down into the sand, and the kisses became more intense. When his caresses reached her breasts she moaned and said, "Charlie?"

"Hmm?"

Melanie popped up. "What are we doing?"

Charlie rolled over. "Being with you takes me back, too. When my brain was in my crotch."

Melanie laughed and sat up. "I got a little wrapped up in the moment myself."

She stood up, brushed off the sand, and held her hand out to a disappointed Charlie. He smiled, took her hand, and pulled himself up. "Guess this means I'm not going to get lucky tonight."

CHAPTER 8

THE NEXT MORNING, Melanie strode through the family room past Ted, asleep in a chair. She turned off the lamp and spoke his name.

He jumped up in his seat and spun around. "Melanie, are you all right?"

"Fine."

"I went back for you a little later, but you were gone."

She sat on the couch. "I spent the night at McNeil's, and Scott drove me home this morning."

"The way I was driving, I could've killed you," he said with remorse.

"And yourself."

He moved to the couch and sat next to her. "I'd like to make it up to you."

Melanie turned to him. "The only way to do that is to support me with the club. Can you do it?"

He put his arm around her and kissed her cheek. "Let's just say I won't oppose you."

———

A FEW MORNINGS later, Melanie went to McNeil's early to meet with the building contractor. He confirmed her plans for the layout and gave her some other exciting ideas for the club. With this, and Ted's approval, she was anxious to get started on the project.

As she readied herself to leave and head back to the Valley for lunch with Sandra, James Mah appeared at the back door and let himself in.

"Hello, Melanie."

"Jesus, you scared me, She exclaimed. "I'm in a hurry. What can I do for you?"

"Word is out you're planning to remodel."

"That's right."

"So you're not taking me up on my offer."

She continued to lock up. "The property is not for sale. I don't care about the money."

"Well, I know that you do care about your husband's career— and that you've been the consummate wife for one of LA's top cops—or not."

She didn't like where this was going. "What are you trying to say, James?"

His eyes narrowed. "I want this property. All of my capital is locked up in a development deal that includes this place. I need it, and you're going to sign it over to me."

Her face flushed. "You're crazy, I—"

"Let me finish. If you don't sell it to me, the police commission may have to find out that the candidate's wife of many years is involved with a business that fronts for a far-reaching methamphetamine ring. I think they would re-consider their assistant chief's promotion, don't you?"

Melanie's heart sped up, and her voice shook. "I don't know what you're talking about."

"Oh, I'm sorry. Let me explain. It's about that investment deal you made with Dean's car dealership last year."

"That's right, a car dealership. I don't know anything about meth."

"You didn't expect him to tell you that part, did you?"

She tried to process the meaning of his words. "I only gave a portion of the cost. He said there were four of us in on the deal."

"Yes, but apparently they all signed it over to you immediately after."

Melanie grabbed for the nearest chair and sat down to absorb what he'd said.

"For all I know, this story is bullshit."

"Oh, I assure you, it's not." James handed her a large manila envelope. "This is a copy of everything I intend to pass on to the commission, and the media."

Melanie jumped up and paced around the room. "That bastard!"

James smirked. "But you have to admit, a charming bastard."

"It wasn't enough that he screwed me, he's giving you the chance, too."

"Well, if it makes you feel any better, he doesn't know anything about my proposition."

"Maybe if he found out he'd—"

"Dean's into me for so much money he wouldn't dare try to bargain on your behalf."

She couldn't hear anymore. "You've said what you came to say. Now get out of my bar."

"Certainly." He gestured toward the envelope. "My phone number is in there. Let me know when you're ready to close the deal."

MELANIE KNEW ONLY one person she could ask for advice, so she arranged to meet Charlie at his house that evening. She paced around the room while he sat at the kitchen table, examining the contents of the envelope.

"Jesus, how could you get yourself involved with those maggots?"

"I met Dean at a Chamber meeting in Encino. Ted was out of town for a few days, and we—" She stopped when she saw him raise his eyebrows. "It wasn't like that. It was all business. The other stuff came later."

He peered at her over his reading glasses with a look of disapproval.

"Oh, really? Care to give me a rundown of your marital indiscretions?"

Charlie cleared his throat and went back to the papers. "There's enough here to implicate you, that's for sure."

"I told you."

"Now tell me you didn't know what Dean was up to."

"I didn't. The business seemed perfectly legitimate, and I've put together enough deals to know the difference."

"From the look of these, he paid you pretty well from the profits."

"It was my way of staying in the business world while still being there for Ted." She plunked down in the chair opposite Charlie. "The funny thing is, I was happier than I'd been in quite a while."

"When did you break off the relationship?"

"About three months ago. Ted was starting to get publicity about his interest in applying for chief. I couldn't afford to have my affair splashed all over TV and the newspapers."

"But you're still getting regular deposits made to your account."

"Of course. That was business. I didn't see anything wrong with having a business venture."

Charlie scoffed. "Especially one so tidy and nicely laundered." He dropped the paperwork, went into the family room, and sat on the couch.

Melanie glared at him, but joined him. "What can I do to stop James?"

"Sell him the damn bar."

"No."

"The slime bag's got you."

"And there's nothing I can do to him legally?"

"Like what?"

Melanie let out a deep sigh. "I'm in trouble aren't I?"

"If you want to stay married to Ted."

How had she gotten to this place? As she sat in silence, the past came flooding up inside of her. "I never did, you know."

Charlie answered matter-of-factly. "Yeah, I know. You wanted Mancini."

"Well, you were already married."

He sloughed it off. "Oh yeah, sure.

"It's true," she said.

"You certainly didn't show it."

"I wasn't interested in just screwing a uniform."

"Jesus. I never saw it."

"You were too busy trying to add me to the notches on your nightstick."

"Funny thing is, it wasn't a line. If I'd thought for a minute I could've really had you I—"

She jumped in. "Would've left your wife and kids?"

He shrugged. "When you walked into the Bronze Anchor the other night, you were exactly as I remembered you. I was so jealous of Ted at that moment."

He scooted over toward her. "But as you spoke, I gazed into your eyes and saw my life in them; empty and full of pain."

He leaned in and brushed her face with his lips. "I could see it. I just didn't realize I was the reason for it."

Melanie pulled back. "Well, not—"

Charlie continued, "I blamed Ted and Mancini, but I know now if I had done the right thing back then, you might not be in this position now."

Melanie bounded to her feet. "Wait a minute! I screw up a marriage and threaten my husband's career, and you're taking the blame for that?"

Charlie sat up and said, "Well I—"

She gathered the papers and her purse into her arms and headed toward the door. "I'll take the blame for my own failures if you don't mind."

Charlie stepped in front of her and grabbed her shoulders. "Mel, wait. I want to make it up to you."

She pulled out of his grasp. "Even if I had spent the last twenty years pining over you, you think you can make up for a lifetime of hurt with a kiss?"

"Of course not, I   "

"Ya know? You're more like Ted than you'd care to believe."

Charlie shook his head and dropped onto the couch, as she opened the door.

"Thanks for the legal advice," she said and walked out.

CHAPTER 9

MELANIE MIGHT HAVE been irritated with Charlie for the things he'd said the night before, but he had confirmed one thing; she needed to sell the bar. After having convinced herself that the club would allow her to re-capture the dreams of her youth, and give her life a new purpose, telling everyone would be painful.

She started by telling Connie that afternoon.

He tried to make her feel better. "I know how tough this is on you, but Benny would be okay with it, really."

Melanie planned to tell Scott and Adriana together that night, so she went down the hall to wait in her office. When she came upon the open back door, she noticed a car pulling up. She did a double-take when she caught a glimpse of Adriana in the passenger seat next to Marco. Hmm. Hadn't that relationship ended when Adriana had learned about Enzo's fate?

Melanie had assumed Adriana would send Marco packing, and come into the bar, so she waited at the door. Instead, she saw Adriana lean over and give him a long kiss. The love scene became more intense, then Adriana got out of the car and made her way to the bar door. Melanie ducked out of sight just before Adriana entered the hallway.

THE NEXT DAY, Charlie walked up to Scott as he sat as his desk in the detective unit. "Come on, I found a lead in the Schneider case."

"Sorry, I have an appointment with a guy said he remembers Mancini."

"I told you we haven't got time for Mancini."

"Since when haven't we got time for a little shopping on duty?"

"Look, I only shop for worthwhile goods. What you're looking for ain't worth shit."

"That's your opinion."

"Yeah, and mine's what's important, cuz I'm the senior man, and I write the shopping list. Roger dat?'

"That's pretty clear."

"Good. Then let's go."

"Can't right now. I'm taking my code 7. Be back in an hour."

Charlie sighed and shook his head, as Scott left.

SCOTT DROVE TO the port, knocked on the door of GLEASON CHARTERS, and found Phil Gleason sitting at his desk.

"I gave a statement to the police back then," Phil said.

"Yeah. You said that Mancini had fired you the day before. You were pissed, but you had an alibi for the night of the murder."

"That's right."

"Anybody else on Mancini's crew have a beef with him?"

"Not that I know of."

"What about Sergio?"

"Hell no. Enzo was tight with him. He even let Sergio take the boat out for personal business sometimes."

Scott had been hoping for more from this guy. "So that's all?"

"Well, I remember that night he fired me I was pretty wasted;

afraid to go home to tell my wife. I knew Mancini hung out at McNeil's Pub on 6th Street, so I went over there to get even by kicking the shit out of him."

"And?" Scott said. "So did you?"

Phil smiled. "Turns out I didn't have to. I only had to suggest to ol' Benny that Mancini might be in bed with his daughter, and he took off and tore into him like a maniac.

"Did you actually see him do it?"

"I followed him outside and saw him go upstairs, but when the shit hit the fan I got the hell out of there. I didn't need any more trouble that day."

"Why didn't you tell this to the police?"

"I would have if they'd try to pin it on me. But I figured the old guy was entitled to protect his daughter. My own daughter was only five at the time, but I understood how he felt."

———

SCOTT ARRANGED TO meet his mother at one of her favorite restaurants in the Valley. It wasn't for a casual lunch. After hearing Phil's story, he had to know if it was true, and she was the only one who could confirm it.

After they were both seated, Scott said, "Thanks for meeting me here, Mom."

"You know I'd never pass up a chance to lunch with you." She placed her napkin on her lap. "So what brings you up here today?"

"You. I wanted to talk to you."

It occurred to her it might have something to do with Adriana. Maybe he'd caught on to her. "Is everything all right?" She asked.

"I'm thinking of dropping the Mancini case."

That sounded promising, she thought. She tried to act nonchalant.

"Really, why?"

"You never told me that Grandpa didn't approve of you seeing Mancini."

"How do you know that?"

"I talked to a guy named Phil Gleason. Know him?"

She shook her head.

"He was there the night Grandpa busted in on you and Mancini. Remember?"

1973

MELANIE AND ENZO were asleep in each other's arms, when Benny burst in to her studio apartment shouting, "Get up you son of a bitch!"

Melanie jumped up. "Daddy, what are you doing?"

"I'm throwing his guinea ass out of your bed." He pulled the sheets off them. "Now, get up and put your clothes on."

"But he loves me, Daddy."

"Maybe loving you and screwing you mean the same thing in Italian, but they're two different things in English."

He grabbed Enzo by the neck, threw him up against the wall, and put a knife to his face. "I don't want to see your face around here again, or they'll be sending you back to sunny Italy in pieces. Capisce?"

1998

SCOTT BROUGHT MELANIE back to his question. "Mom? Did it happen?"

She nodded.

"And he didn't have an alibi for the time of the murder?"

Melanie looked up with tears in her eyes and shook her head. "In twenty-five years I've never said it out loud."

Scott sat back in his chair. "But you never forgave him either."

"No," she whispered and took a sip of water.

"So why did you reopen the bar?"

"I thought if I did, I could make peace with him, with myself."

CONNIE WAS NEXT on Scott's list, so he invited him over to watch a ballgame. Scott handed Connie a beer and sat down in his recliner.

"Ya know, Mom didn't mention that Grandpa hated Mancini."

"He'd seen guys like him pass through the bar for years. It wasn't what he wanted for his daughter. Matter of fact, it was his worst nightmare." Connie took a swig of beer. "I figured it wouldn't last, but Benny couldn't wait it out."

"Are you saying he did it?"

"Hell, he was mad enough. I went looking for him that night, but I never found him."

Scott stood up and stared out a window. "Jesus, I wish I'd never started this."

"Then go to that office of yours, and file those records back where they belong, in 1973."

CONNIE ALWAYS TOOK a break from his shift by smoking his cigar on a bench outside next to the front door. Saturday night was no different. It wasn't known if he had noticed the two gang-bangers walk by on their way to the store next door, because a spray of gunfire from a passing car blew Connie off the bench. By the time

Adriana got to him after hearing the shots, he was dead.

When Scott arrived, police, paramedics, and the coroner's office vehicles clogged the street. He spotted Charlie standing next to Adriana, who was still in a state of shock. She answered questions in between sobs.

"Looks like a gang hit," Charlie said. "You noticed much gang activity around here?"

"The usual," Scott said, as he comforted Adriana.

"Why would they do this to him?" she cried. "He never hurt them."

"They weren't after him. They probably wanted the gangbangers walking by the bar."

"This is terrible," she said.

Charlie took Scott aside. "We've got her statement. Why don't you take her home? I'll get somebody else to help with this one."

"I'll take her home, but I'm coming back."

CHARLIE AND SCOTT worked nothing but Connie's case for the next couple of weeks. They talked to the two gangbangers who were at the scene. They knocked on doors up and down the street, and in surrounding neighborhoods. Charlie hit up two of his snitches. They came up empty. There was nothing left to do, but bury Connie the way he had always said he wanted.

Melanie, Ted, Scott, Adriana, and Charlie stood on the deck of a freighter in the harbor. They comforted each other as the minister spoke over Connie's remains. When he finished, he gave the urn to Melanie who opened it and released the contents into the water. "Smooth sailing, friend."

From there, they all retreated to the bar for a toast to Connie.

Before the toast, Melanie took Charlie aside in the back room and whispered, "Thanks for coming today."

"I've known Connie for over twenty years, too."

"I know. But I've been wanting to apologize for going off on you that day when you were just trying to comfort me."

Charlie smiled and shrugged. "Hey, I took a lot more abuse than that from you at Harbor, and it never stopped me from going back for more."

"It's just that I'd never realized how many other lives have been affected by my marrying Ted for the wrong reasons, and I—"

They were interrupted by Ted's voice from the bar where he, Scott, and Adriana were ready to give the toast. Scott poured as Melanie and Charlie joined them.

With glasses held high, they all said, "To Connie. A hell of a guy."

Melanie swallowed her drink and said, "I have an announcement. In light of everything that's happened, I've decided to sell the bar."

"But Mom, are you sure?"

"Yes. I should have put it up for sale weeks ago."

Ted reached out and pulled her to him. "I know how many plans you had for the remodel. I hope you're not doing this on my account. You know I was—"

"No. It's for the best. And the good thing is," she glanced over at Charlie. "I've already had a great offer."

The group became silent.

"So," she said, changing the subject, "are you guys any closer to the gangbangers who shot Connie?"

Charlie said, "There's no evidence that it was a gang hit."

"But those guys were standing right there," Adriana said.

Ted downed his champagne. "What have you found?"

"Nobody's taking credit for this one."

Scott explained. "There was no call-out at the scene, and no chatter about it later."

Adriana seemed confused. "What does that mean?"

"You have to understand the gang mentality," Ted said. "There's no point in a hit unless their rivals know it was them."

"So what does that leave us with?" Melanie asked.

Ted answered. "It leaves us to assume that whoever fired that rifle probably got the man he was after."

CHAPTER 10

WITH CONNIE'S MURDER still unsolved, her suspicions about Adriana, and James Mah's threat hanging over her head, Melanie couldn't face the emotional job of packing up the bar by herself, so she asked Sandra to help. They arrived ready for work, wearing jeans and carrying boxes. Sandra jumped in by clearing off the table tops.

"So how do you want to organize this stuff?" she said.

But Melanie's thoughts were elsewhere, so instead of answering her question, she told her she had seen Adriana with another man.

"You didn't trust her from the minute she walked in the door." Sandra pointed to the back entrance.

"I know, but I kept hoping I was wrong for Scott's sake."

"What are you going to do?"

"I asked Charlie to run a check on her. Including her visa status."

"You'd send her to jail?"

"In a heartbeat."

"I give you credit. You've got balls."

"If I really had a set, I'd tell James what to do with himself and open my club."

She started to gather things from behind the bar. "I can't believe

McNeil's Pub will be gone for good. It's where I grew up."

"I don't think I really realized that my mother was dead until my brother and I signed the escrow papers and moved her things out of the house."

Charlie called out from the open back door. "Hey, anybody here?"

Melanie recognized his voice and walked in the back to let him in. "Charlie, come in."

"I took a chance on finding you here."

"I thought I'd better get this stuff out of here as soon as possible."

He nodded and followed her back.

"Oh, Charlie. This is my good friend, Sandra."

The two exchanged niceties.

"Sorry to interrupt," Charlie said. "but I need to ask you a couple of questions about Connie."

"Sure."

"I've been going through his bank statements."

"What for?"

"Somebody wanted him dead, and until we find out why, we won't know who."

Melanie smiled. "Well, they certainly didn't kill him for his money. He didn't have much."

"Not until recently, anyway." Charlie said. "Was he a gambler?"

"Connie?" She said with surprise. "No. He wouldn't even bet on the World Series. He thought gambling was for suckers."

"Any wealthy relatives die lately?"

"Not that I know of. Why?"

"Because he deposited fifty thousand dollars cash into his account a couple of weeks ago."

"Really?"

"Yup."

"That's strange."

Charlie looked around the bar in disarray. "Pretty tough day, huh?"

She nodded. "I'll get through it."

"Well, you take care." Charlie said and made his way to the back door.

Melanie trailed behind him. "Charlie?"

"Yeah?"

She took him aside and spoke in a low voice. "I want you to know that I have thought a lot about you over the years, and I'm really glad we've had a chance to know each other again. Even under these lousy circumstances."

He placed his hand on her arm and squeezed it. Melanie gazed up at the yearning in his face, and she covered his hand with hers.

"Mel, I wan—"

Then Sandra walked in on them with a question for Melanie.

Charlie cleared his throat. "Well, thanks for the info. You take care. Uh, you too. Sandra."

Sandra and Melanie went back to work in silence. After an awkward moment, Sandra said. "You know, I wouldn't go out with a cop again to save my alimony, but I would kill to have Charlie look at me just once, the way he looks at you."

———

TWO DAYS LATER, Melanie's phone rang. "Hi, it's Charlie."

"Hey, what's up?"

"I came up with a lead on Adriana. You able to take a ride to Santa Barbara on Saturday?"

"Santa Barbara, huh? I'll make time."

"Good. Where can I meet you?"

At the McDonalds, right before the northbound onramp of the 101."

"Ten okay?"

"Perfect."

After picking her up, Charlie explained they were going to The Capri Deli, where Adriana had worked before showing up in San Pedro. They filled the hour-and-fifteen-minute ride with small talk, as if they both feared broaching subjects too difficult for them to handle.

They strolled into the small store, trying not to make their intentions obvious to the line of customers waiting at the check-out and deli counters. When the lines had thinned, Charlie approached a man in his fifties. "We're looking for Mr. or Mrs. Frank Bettini."

"I'm Frank. What can I do for you?"

Charlie explained the reason for their visit, and Frank called his wife before directing them into an office. Once inside the cramped space, Charlie brought up Adriana.

The wife, Anna, didn't hesitate before filling them in. "Frank invited her for a vacation, and they stayed almost three months. Her and that Marco guy."

Frank threw her an irritated look. "My cousin called from Italy and asked if her Greek husband's niece could stay with us. I like keeping in touch with family over there, so I said sure. How'd I know she'd bring that deadbeat boyfriend?"

"What do you know about him?"

"Apparently he's her stepbrother, Anna said. "Only I accidently walked in on them, and caught them carrying sibling love a little too far."

"All I know is she was willing to help out around here, but he never seemed to have the time; always off somewhere," Frank said.

Melanie spoke up. "Did they tell you where they were going when they left?"

"No. I figured since their visas were up, they went back home."

Anna had the last word. "Yeah, with my jewelry and three thousand dollars from our safe."

———

AFTER THE BETTINI'S officially reported the crime, Santa Barbara Police Department put a warrant out on Adriana and Marco. Charlie notified Harbor Division robbery detectives, Previn and McCall, of Adriana's whereabouts in San Pedro. They wasted no time before arresting her and taking her to Harbor Station.

Charlie called Melanie, told her what had just gone down and asked her to meet him and Scott at the station. He hadn't mentioned to Scott the suspect that they were about to interrogate was Adriana. So when Scott saw her sitting there with the detectives, he didn't know what to think.

"Adriana, what are doing here?" He glared at Charlie. "What the hell is going on?"

Adriana cried out. "They want to put me in jail."

"On what charge?" Scott said.

"Grand Theft," Detective Previn said.

"Of what?"

Detective McCall came forward. "We picked her up on a Santa Barbara PD warrant. According to a Mr. and Mrs. Bettini of the Capri Deli, she and her friend, Marco, stole some jewelry and three thousand dollars from their safe while they were staying with them."

Scott looked at Adriana. "Who are these Bettini's?"

"Distant relatives."

"This Marco guy came with her from Greece, but has kept a low profile here in Pedro," Previn said.

McCall jumped in. "So low that we need Ms. Dimakos's help locating him."

Melanie slipped into the doorway unnoticed.

Scott had had enough. "She doesn't know where he is."

Melanie declared from the back of the room. "That's not true, Scott."

He spun around to face his mother.

"She's been seeing him all this time."

"They called you, too?"

"No, honey. I called them."

Scott lashed out at Melanie. "You did this?" He took a breath and said to the detectives, "Can we have the room?"

Previn and McCall turned to leave.

Scott peered over at Charlie. "You too."

Behind closed doors, Scott glared at his mother. "I should've known. You were determined to get rid of her, weren't you?"

Melanie hated herself at that moment for betraying him and couldn't speak.

He turned to Adriana. "Do you know where Marco is?"

She didn't answer, so he asked Melanie, "How did you know about those Santa Barbara people?"

Melanie answered in a loud whisper. "Charlie ran a check on her for me."

"Un-fucking-believable! You two are a pair."

He eyed Adriana. "You stole money from your own relatives?"

"Marco and I were broke, and we needed to get down here."

"When's the last time you saw him?"

"Last week."

"You told me you barely knew him, and you hadn't seen him since that night we—since that night."

Melanie wished she could wrap her arms around him and make the hurt go away. But she blamed herself, and she'd be lucky if he ever talked to her again.

"Why don't you tell them where he is?" He said to Adriana with resignation. "They won't be so hard on you."

"No."

"You'd take the rap for him?"

She nodded.

He rubbed his neck. "What were we all about?"

Adriana peered up at Melanie. "I had to make her pay."

"You would've married me for revenge?"

She stared at the wall in silence, and Scott walked out of the room, leaving the two women alone.

Melanie stood up to leave, but Adriana stopped her. "You don't know what it's like to have nothing of your own, always somebody's leftovers. To not have what's rightfully yours."

"Maybe not, but I do know what it is to not be able to have the thing you want most. To settle for what's leftover. I know what it is to charm someone who loves you into making up for that, because I did it."

"So, we are alike."

Melanie glared at her and nodded. "That's why you should have known I would never stand by and watch you destroy the most important thing in the world to me."

SCOTT TOOK THE next few days off. He had plenty of sick days available, and the way he felt, it wasn't a lie. He likened his pain to a run-in with a Mack truck. He ignored all phone calls and tried to work it out of his system on the treadmill. Despite what had happened, he loved Adriana, missed coming home to her and having her in his bed. He tried to toss her things away, but somehow, they were a comfort, as if she were still there.

He couldn't face Charlie and didn't want to talk to his mother, because he was still pissed at them for conspiring against him. He didn't even want to call his friends. How could he tell them about the humiliation he'd suffered?

By the third day, he began to realize that no one was to blame, but himself. *How could I let that bitch use me? Mom and Charlie saw through her and tried to warn me, but I was thinking with my dick.* After a few days of admitting he had fucked up, he went back to work and answered his mother's calls.

WITH NO GOOD leads to Connie's killer, Scott and Charlie made the rounds of the local bars in search of one of Connie's buddies. Scott spotted him perched on a barstool wearing his tattered sea captain's hat.

He hopped up on the stool next to him. "Arthur? Recognize me? I'm Scott Swain from McNeil's Pub. Benny's grandson."

Arthur turned toward him and squinted. "Oh yeah. How the fuck are ya, kid? When you gonna open McNeil's again? This place is a dump."

"My Mom's selling it."

"Oh, that's a damn shame."

"Yeah, it is. Hey, we wanted to ask you a few questions about Connie. That okay with you?" He pointed to Charlie. "This is my partner, Charlie Moore."

"Sure. You arrest those mother fucking assholes who shot him yet?"

"No, not yet. We need some more information. Did Connie mention anything about coming into quite a bit of money lately?"

Arthur shifted on his stool and took gulp of from his glass.

"Scott noticed his hesitation. "No matter what you say, you can only help Connie now. You can't hurt him."

"Well, he said he saw something a long time ago, and some fucker was going to have to pay him some big money to keep his mouth shut."

Scott caught Charlie's eye. "Did he say what it was he knew?"

"No, but he said he waited a long time to be able to collect on it."

The pair thanked Arthur and turned to walk out. "Okay," Charlie said to Scott, "tell me what you found out about the Mancini case."

Scott filled him in on what he'd learned.

"So," Charlie said, "what was Connie waiting for all that time?

"You got me."

"Let's start with the elusive Sergio," Charlie said. "See if he even had fifty thousand to protect his ass."

Scott's mind had wandered. "Jesus," he said, "I knew Connie saw something that night. Now at least I know it wasn't Benny. And all these years Mom blamed him."

MELANIE PICKED UP the ringing phone and heard Scott say he was on his way to see her. He hadn't said why. Why would he come all the way up here on a work day? He had sounded strange on the phone, and she worried it might have something to do with Adriana. They had only spoken briefly since the arrest, and she wasn't convinced he had forgiven her. While she waited, she made some iced tea, his favorite soft drink, and tried to busy herself.

He came in the back door. "Mom? Where are you?" With no response, he wandered to the back of the house and found her in the workout room.

Melanie stepped down off the bike when she saw him and led him into the kitchen, where she poured him a glass of tea.

"Is something wrong? she said.

"No. Not really."

She had to ask. "Does this have anything to do with Adriana?"

"No. Well, kinda, in an indirect way."

She sat down at the table and motioned to him to do the same. "Well, what is it, honey? You seem upset."

"Mom, I found out today that Connie probably knew all along who killed Mancini— and it wasn't Grandpa."

THE NEXT DAY, Melanie cancelled her appointments and drove to Long Beach. She drove into the parking lot of All Soul's Cemetery and made her way to her father and mother's gravesites. As she placed flowers near his headstone for the first time, regret overwhelmed her. So much time wasted for what she'd thought he'd done. How could she have let him die shouldering her unsubstantiated accusations? She brushed away the tears streaming from her eyes.

"Oh, Daddy. I'm so sorry."

MELANIE NOW KNEW what she had to do. She had to keep her father's bar at all costs. She called Dean and scheduled a meeting with him and a friend of hers, a notary public, at a small bistro in the Valley. Melanie arrived at the meeting with the appropriate papers to sign in order to remove her as owner of the auto dealership.

When all the t's had been crossed, and i's had been dotted, Melanie took some folded bills from her purse and handed them to her friend. "I appreciate your doing this for me."

"You're quite welcome. Have a good night."

Dean watched her walk away and turned to Melanie. "Happy now?"

She ignored the remark. "I want any evidence showing I ever had anything to do with that dealership destroyed. My attorney will be contacting you."

"All right, all right. I'll take care of it."

"And you can deliver a message to your friend, James. Tell him I have no intention of selling him my property, now or ever."

Dean began to squirm. "But he won't back down. I know him. He'll do what he said he would."

Melanie stood up and slung her purse strap over her shoulder. "Let him. Just remember, after he broadcasts what he knows, I'll have nothing to lose—but you will."

CHAPTER 11

CHARLIE AND SCOTT'S search for Sergio began with a woman named Estella Hernandez. According to the 1973 files, she had been listed as Sergio's girlfriend at the time of the murder. They found her still living in the area and parked themselves on her street, adjacent to her known residence.

From their vantage point, they had a perfect view of the small apartment building. After sitting there for a couple of hours, Scott saw a car pull into one of the carports outside the building.

"Look," he nudged Charlie. "Could that be her?"

They watched an attractive woman in her forties get out and gather her bags from the trunk, and head for the building.

Charlie whistled his approval. They jumped out of their car and followed her.

"Estella Hernandez?" Scott called out.

Her head shot up. "Yes?" she said.

"Uh, didn't mean to scare you, but—"

She shifted the bags in her arms. "Who are you and what do you want?"

Charlie flashed his badge at her. "LAPD."

"What's wrong? Is it my son?'

"Your son?" Scott said.

"No, ma'am. Nothing like that. We're here about Sergio Oliva. Do you know where we might be able to find him?"

"You still looking for him?"

"Yeah. So you remember the 1973 case. Have you seen him lately?"

"No."

"When's the last time?"

"Long time ago." She unlocked her apartment door. "We were a couple back then, but I don't know any more now than I did before."

She stepped inside, set the packages on the floor, and pulled the door to her.

Scott made a last-ditch effort. "Did he ever say anything about getting rid of Mancini?"

"Hey, I don't know anything about that or Sergio. Now go away and leave me alone," she said, as she shut the door in their faces.

Charlie shook his head on their way back to the car. "Either she was a pretty lousy lay, or he is guilty as hell. I can't believe he wouldn't have come back for more of that if he was in town."

Scott smiled. "Pretty romantic notion coming from you, don't ya think?"

Charlie shrugged. "I have my moments."

———

TWO DAYS LATER, Charlie walked up to Scott's desk. "I just got a call from a Tony Hernandez.

"Who's he?'

"Estella Hernandez' son."

Scott looked up at Charlie. "He ever hear of Sergio?"

"Sergio's his ol' man."

Charlie had found out Tony was doing time at the county jail fa-
cility, so they drove there and asked to speak to him. They introduced
themselves to a nineteen-year old man with a mustache and beard
and asked why he'd called them.

"I can't stand seeing my mother cry, and she was crying her eyes
out yesterday."

"That's the reason you want to rat on Sergio? Because he made
your mother cry?"

"The son of a bitch has been dropping in and out of our lives
for years. He drops in when he's horny and broke and leaves her a
couple of days later with nothing but a sore back and an empty bank
account."

Charlie glanced at Scott with a smug smile.

Tony continued, "I know she did it for me. She thought it was
better to have a part-time father than no father."

"So, when he was playing father," Scott said, "he put you on his
knee and told you how he whacked Mancini?"

"Of course not," Tony said.

Scott became impatient with him. "Well, then what did he do?"

Charlie signaled for Scott to take it easy. "So, what do you know,
kid?"

"Some of the guys in here." Tony put his head down and hesitated. "They say you could maybe help me out with my trial if I help
you."

Charlie gave Scott a knowing look. "What are you in for?"

"Armed robbery."

Charlie paced around. "I really hate little pukes like you, but if
you got something, I'll talk to the DA. That's all I can promise; that
I'll talk to him. Now what about Mancini?"

"Mom said Mancini never suspected that Sergio was bringing

dope in on that boat."

"He must've had help with the operation," Scott said.

Tony shrugged. "Some relative in Mexico, and some guy who set up the buys here."

"Did you ever hear a name?"

"No. Just that he was a greedy bastard and Sergio didn't trust him—I think he was in the military."

"And?"

"And that's all."

Charlie slapped his knee. "Shit. We could've guessed all that. I'm not asking the DA to stick his neck out for nothing."

Tony smirked. "You want to find him, don't you?"

"Where is he?" Scott said.

"Well, I don't know, but I do know somebody who does."

Charlie jumped up. "All right, man. Let's get you to a telephone."

SCOTT HADN'T TALKED to his father since Adriana's arrest and hadn't shared much with him about the Mancini case. Since he had to go to Parker Center in downtown LA for a meeting that week, he stopped in Ted's office, and brought him up to date on both.

"Yeah, that Tony was a piece of work," Scott said. "So much for protecting his old lady. He was just hoping to cut a deal with the DA."

"Just be glad you found him. When's the meeting going down?"

"Not for a few days. Apparently the contact is out of town." Scott sighed. "Christ, I'm sorry I got involved in this whole thing."

Ted leaned back in his chair and clamped his hands behind his head. "I told you to stay in the Valley, but you had to experience the south end."

"How'd I know Mom's past would jump up and bite me on the ass?"

"It hasn't been easy for her either. This news about Connie is killing her. She trusted him all these years."

Scott mumbled, "We all did."

"She's more worried about you, though. You mean more to her than anything, and she blames herself for this thing with the girl."

"That wasn't her fault."

Ted crossed his hands in his lap and smiled. "From what I could see you got your money's worth."

Scott grinned and winked. "Oh yeah." After a deep breath, his mood changed. "I was going to marry her."

Ted leaned forward and spoke in earnest, "Scott, if she didn't love you, you're lucky you found out before you married her. Believe me, it'd be like getting kicked in the balls every day of your life."

CHAPTER 12

MELANIE HAD RESUMED planning her remodel of the bar and spent at least one day a week there to meet with workmen. She hadn't stopped the delivery of the local paper, so she made a point of checking the business news before tossing it out each week.

As she thumbed through the last edition, she did a double-take when she saw a picture of James Mah above the caption, "LOCAL BUSINESSMAN DIES: VICTIM OF A HIT AND RUN."

In shock, she scanned the article in a hurry and learned that an unidentified person had gotten away. After absorbing what she'd read, she remembered what she'd told Dean, "— After he broadcasts what he knows, I'll have nothing to lose—but you will." She shook her head. "Dean." Could he have gone to those extremes? She didn't want to know, but a weight had been lifted from her, and she sighed with relief.

———

THE FOLLOWING SATURDAY, Scott and Charlie arrived at a San Pedro coffee shop in plain clothes, sat on counter stools and waited. Scott had taken a sip of his coffee when he spotted a guy who fit Sergio's description, and he made eye contact with the waitress behind the counter. She nodded, and the detectives followed Sergio to a booth in the back.

Scott slipped in the seat across from him, and Charlie nudged Sergio over toward the wall.

Sergio twitched. "Hey, what do you guys want? I ain't got no money."

"You Oliva?" Scott asked.

"Name's Santos."

"That's funny. Waitress says your name is Sergio Oliva."

Sergio twisted in his seat. "Well, she was wrong."

"A dirtbag by any other name—," Charlie placed a picture of Mancini on the table in front of him.—"Is still a dirtbag."

Sergio jumped up and climbed over the top of the seat, but Charlie grabbed the tail of his jacket, while Scott ran over to tackle him. Scott then held him down while Charlie handcuffed him.

"Serge, my man, we're not as goddamned young as we used to be, huh? That's why I travel with Scott here. You should remember that."

"We just want to ask you a few questions. After all, the detectives never had a chance to do that in '73." Scott stood him up. "We've got a car outside to transport you to Harbor Station. We'll all be more comfortable there."

THEY ARRIVED AT the station and led Sergio into an interview room, where they all sat at the table.

"Talk to us," Charlie said.

Sergio sat with his arms crossed. "I don't know nothin'.

"Now, if we thought that, we wouldn't be wasting our time with you, would we?" Scott said.

Charlie leaned back in his chair. "Maybe if we tell you a couple of things we know, it'll jog your memory. First of all, we know you were using Enzo's boat to transport contraband from Mexico without his knowledge, and that you were unloading a shipment the night he died. And we know that you disappeared before the police could talk to you." Charlie leaned forward. "Now, you've got to admit that puts you pretty high on the list of suspects."

"I didn't kill him," Sergio insisted.

Scott said, "We sort of expected you to say that. So prove it."

Sergio shrugged. "I ain't got to. You got to prove I did it, and it don't seem like you can."

Scott and Charlie exchanged glances.

"Okay," Scott tried another approach, "what do you know about the murder of Connie Conroy?"

Sergio sneered. "Who the hell is Connie Conroy?"

Charlie had had enough. "All right, let's say you didn't kill Mancini, but you know who did. Would you tell us?"

Sergio smirked. "You ain't got enough money."

"So it's money that's kept you under wraps all these years. How much?"

Sergio stared at the ceiling.

Charlie stood up and paced around the room. "It doesn't matter. You're right. We don't have enough—but maybe we have something else worth almost as much. We know that your son, Tony, stands to do some hard time for a couple of robberies. And we might be able to arrange it so he gets the minimum sentence."

Charlie sighed and began to play the guilt angle. "Christ, man. I know how it is. I wasn't always there for my kids, and I'd give anything to find a way to make it up to them." Charlie cleared his throat. "This is your chance to do this for Tony."

Sergio squinted, but said nothing.

Scott added. "Besides, you may have been able to stay lost for twenty-five years, but not anymore. If you don't tell us what you know now, we'll be up your ass everywhere you go."

"Come on, Serge. Do your kid a favor," Charlie reasoned.

———

THAT SAME MORNING, Melanie stood in front of her full-length mirror, slipped her blouse over her head, and smoothed it over her slacks. She admired the outfit and went over to sit at her dressing table. She finished styling her hair and dug through her purse to find the perfect lipstick color to match her clothes.

After pulling out two tubes of the wrong color, she remembered the last time she used it had been in the car. It wasn't unusual for the tubes to fall out of her purse when she was driving, so she walked out to the garage and opened the passenger door of her car. She put her hand under the seat and felt around on the floor.

She came up with a pack of tissues, a nail file, and her holstered .38 caliber snub-nose revolver, but no lipstick. The gun had been in her car for many years, on Ted's insistence that she have something to defend herself when driving alone at night. She put the tissues and nail file in the glove compartment and the gun back under the seat.

It occurred to her the lipstick might be in Ted's car, so she searched under his seat, and found it there; along with a handwritten note on a piece of paper. She didn't recognize the scrawl, but it read, "Let's meet at the same spot, but don't keep me waiting this time. I promise you Melanie will never find out."

"What the hell?" Melanie thought. He's cheating on me? All these years, the only good thing about this marriage, besides Scott, has been his loyalty. Without that, what's left?

SCOTT AND CHARLIE prepared to record Sergio's statement about the night Mancini had died.

Charlie pressed the record button and adjusted himself in his chair. "Okay, start from the beginning."

"Well," Sergio began. "I'd been hauling shit from Mexico on his boat for about a year. That dumb dago never even knew it. I'd met this sailor in Long Beach who had some connections on the street, and I knew a guy in Mexico. We figured we could make a couple of trips and make some fast cash. But hell, it was too easy to quit. Man, we were rollin' in the dough.

"Couple of times, though, we had some close calls, and I thought we should lay off for a while. But that fucking swabbie didn't want to stop. He didn't give a shit about my job.

"Well, the last time, Mancini had left me the boat while he went out of town for a couple of weeks. We thought we could get one more haul in before he came back. But he got back before us and showed up on the dock while we was unloading."

1973

MANCINI WATCHED AS Sergio unloaded bricks of marijuana from the boat to a van. "What the hell are you doing?"

"Shit," Sergio said under his breath.

Mancini hopped aboard, walked over to the kilos, picked them up, and smelled them. "Are you crazy? We both could go to jail!"

He dropped the contraband, grabbed Sergio by the collar, and punched him in the face. "You stupid Mexican. I never should've trusted you with my business. Without it, I don't eat."

Sergio rubbed his jaw. "I can explain."

"Don't explain anything to me. Explain to the police. I'm not going to lose my visa for you."

CHAPTER 13

1998

SERGIO LOOKED UP at Charlie. "Mancini started to reach for the radio. But before he could make the call, the sailor came up behind and stabbed him in the back."

There it was; proof of Benny's innocence. A surge of relief washed over Scott.

"He told me I better keep my mouth shut or we could go to jail for murder, since we were committing a felony with the drugs when it happened. But later, I felt bad about Mancini and started thinking I could make a deal with the police if I snitched on the sailor. He must've read my mind, so he gave me thirty grand to keep my mouth shut and disappear.

That was a lot of money back then, and I didn't have no other offers. That's when I found out that he hadn't been a sailor for a while. Turns out he was one of you guys."

"You mean he was a cop?"

"Yeah. Worked at this station. You two know him." He grinned at Scott. "Name's Ted Swain."

Scott paced around the men's room while Charlie tried to calm him down. "Jesus, kid. I'm sorry. I know it's hard on you, but it's not easy for me, either. He and I were pretty close in those days, and I had no clue that he was dirty."

Scott kept taking deep breaths to offset the waves of nausea.

Charlie handed him a cup of water and turned the faucet on. "Here, drink this, and throw some water on your face."

Scott obeyed as a million crazy thoughts swirled around in his brain. "So it was Dad that Connie saw that night. No wonder he kept it to himself all those years."

Charlie added. "He knew Benny thought of Ted like a son." He shook his head and sighed. "Shit."

Scott struggled to absorb this new realty about his father. "Oh my God, my mother."

———

LATER THAT MORNING, Melanie fumed in silence over the note she'd found, while nursing a cup of coffee at the kitchen table. Ted walked through wearing golf attire on his way to the garage. "I'm leaving now."

Melanie played dumb. "Who are you golfing with today?"

"A business associate invited me to his club in Calabasas."

"What about dinner?"

"We'll probably have an early dinner after the round."

"Okay. See ya later."

As soon as Ted walked out, Melanie grabbed her purse and listened for Ted's car to pull out of the garage. When it did, she ran out to the garage, jumped into her car, and sped down the street until she had him in her sights. From there she maintained a safe distance be-hind as she tailed him to the 405 Freeway south entrance. She knew then he wasn't going west to Calabasas.

Ted took her down the familiar route on the 405 toward the Harbor Freeway. Somehow, she hadn't figured the other woman would live in the South Bay area. Then to her surprise they were heading for San Pedro.

As they approached the exit, he looked in his rear-view mirror, and she flinched. He began his exit, another car cut Melanie off, and they rolled into a lot of traffic at the end of the ramp. When the light turned green, Ted pulled forward, but Melanie found herself stuck behind a couple of cars, and she struggled to keep her eyes on his car while weaving in between lanes.

Afraid he would see her when he checked his rear-view mirror, she hung back as he turned into the lot of an abandoned warehouse, parked his car and disappeared into the building. By now, curiosity had gotten the better of her, and she couldn't imagine that he would be meeting a lover in this smelly old place.

Melanie drove around to the side of the building, pulled up next to Ted's car, and got out of hers. The sound of a fog horn in the distance caused her to stop and gaze at her surroundings, and she shuddered. The back door had been broken into, so she made her way in on tiptoes.

She eased down a hallway, listening for voices, but heard none. After noticing a catwalk above, she climbed up and made her way toward a large open room, where she spotted Ted down below pacing, and looking out the window.

CHARLIE AND SCOTT had wired Sergio and accompanied him to his meeting with Ted at the warehouse, followed by two black-and-whites for backup. Charlie and Scott hid in the backseat of Sergio's car as Sergio drove up to the front of the building and got out.

"Stay cool now, Serge," Charlie warned.

Inside, Melanie continued to watch an anxious Ted. She saw his attention turn toward the sound of another pair of footsteps approaching the room. To her surprise, he pulled his gun out of his back pocket and took aim. Melanie could tell by Ted's expression and body language that whoever was walking into that room was in trouble. She let out a scream, two shots rang out, and a man she'd never seen fell to the ground.

Ted jerked and pointed his gun toward her above him.

"Melanie!"

Scott and Charlie drew their guns outside at the sound of the shots, and headed toward the back of the building. When Scott turned the corner, he caught a glimpse of Melanie's car. "Wait! What the hell?"

Charlie stopped.

"My Mother's in there."

"What?"

"Look." Scott pointed. "There's her car."

"Fuck."

Scott moved toward the entrance "I've got to get to her."

"No." Charlie pressed his earphone into his ear. "Listen. I hear something."

Melanie eased down from her perch in the catwalk.

"What are you doing here?" Ted shouted.

She ran over to Sergio. "My God, Ted. Look what you've done."

Ted followed her to where Sergio lay bleeding from a head wound, and gestured for her to move away from him. "He'll be dead soon."

"But why?' Why would you do this?"

Ted ignored her. "How did you find me here?"

"I followed you."

"What for?"

"I, uh, found the note from your girlfriend."

"What girlfriend?"

Melanie handed him the crumpled note. "Who is she?"

Ted scanned it. "This is from Connie. That son of a bitch has been waiting all these years for your old man to die so he could milk me."

"What are you talking about?" She pointed to Sergio. "Who is that?"

He sighed. "You don't know. You don't know what's been going on. It's Sergio."

"Sergio?" I don't understand!"

Ted shook his head slowly and lowered his gun. "I never meant to kill Mancini. But he caught us with the contraband, and I had no choice."

Melanie's thoughts bounced around her mind trying to absorb what she had just heard.

"My God," she said when it came to her. "It was you. "You were Sergio's partner." She didn't get it. "But why kill him after all these years?"

"Scott was getting close to finding him, and I couldn't take that chance."

"And Connie?"

"He's always known. I had to kill him. He was going to ruin everything I've worked so hard for." His voice softened. "I did it all for you, you know?"

"For me?"

"I had to make up for Mancini. I had to give you a reason to love me, but it wasn't enough, was it?"

This was all too much, and Melanie didn't know what to say.

"Was it?" Ted yelled, and raised his gun.

She stared into his eyes and whispered. "You let me think it was Daddy all those years."

"Yeah, and you pretended to be faithful to me."

"I'm sorry. The thing with Dean just happened."

"How many others were there before that sleaze?"

"There weren't—"

"Do you hate me that much?"

"I don't hate you."

"Who else knew your dirty little secret?"

"Nobody."

He shrugged. "I'm sure Dean bragged to his slimy friends. They all knew you were fucking him!"

Outside, the audio feed had started breaking up, and Scott couldn't stand still. He finally announced, "I'm going in."

Charlie grabbed his arm and attempted to hold him back, but Scott pulled out of his grasp, ran toward the door, and drew his gun. Charlie signaled to him to wait while he grabbed his weapon. Scott complied, and on Charlie's signal the two pushed through the door.

Melanie and Ted turned, startled, as Scott stumbled over Sergio's body in the doorway. Ted aimed his gun at the intruders, then grabbed Melanie and held her like a shield in front of him. Melanie gasped as she stood in the middle of the three guns.

"You didn't tell me you brought backup, honey." Ted said.

"I didn't know they were out there."

"She didn't know, Dad. Come on, let her go."

"I thought you guys knew better than to rush in on a hostage situation," Ted said. "Especially you, Charlie, one of the best goddamn street cops I know."

"What are you doing chief? Melanie could get hurt here. Could you live with yourself if that happens?"

"It's up to you. All you gotta do is put your guns down."

Scott and Charlie held their positions.

Ted thrust Melanie forward in anger and screamed at Scott. "This is your mother!"

Melanie jerked out of his grasp, prompting Scott and Charlie to lunge forward. In the scuffle, Scott landed on the floor, and Charlie grabbed for Ted's gun. The two struggled for it, causing Charlie to drop his gun.

Ted kicked it away and managed to yank his own weapon from Charlie. With Charlie on the floor looking up at him, Ted aimed the gun at Charlie's head.

Scott, now on his feet, directed his gun at his father. "No, Dad. Don't!"

Ted eyeballed Scott. "Go ahead son. Pull the trigger."

Scott stared at his father, clutching his gun with his quivering hands, but he couldn't bring himself to do it.

Seconds later, a shot rang out, from behind them, and Ted dropped to the floor, a bullet in his head. Scott and Charlie whirled around where Melanie stood there, her face deadly pale, gripping a smoking gun.

CHAPTER 14

WITHIN MINUTES, BREAKING news could be seen on every LA area TV station and in last editions of newspapers.

"Wife shoots LAPD Assistant Chief in standoff!"

"Son cracks Assistant Chief's 1973 Cold-Case Murder!"

News vans and reporters swarmed Harbor station, the Swains' neighborhood, Scott's apartment, and McNeil's. They remained there for three days, harassed anyone they could find to make a statement about the family and the incident; looking to sensationalize any piece of information. Finally, three days after the incident. Plain-clothes detectives escorted Melanie and Scott to a hotel in a nearby town in the middle of the night. But the frenzy continued until after the day of Ted's private burial. Only Scott and Melanie attended. She refused to allow Scott to face the day alone.

SIX WEEKS LATER, Melanie still struggled with the outcome of the shooting. Recurring nightmares of the scene robbed her of sleep. Her attention span had shrunk along with her appetite. Worst of all, guilt had kept her from talking to Scott since the funeral, despite her worry about the incident's effect on him.

She rarely ventured outside, because the press still bombarded her with questions. Just when she thought it safe to pick up newspapers in her driveway, two men, one with a camera, appeared out of nowhere.

"Mrs. Swain, I'm Bob Mandano from the six o'clock news."

She raised her hand and signaled the men to stop. "Why are you people still here?" she cried.

"I was hoping that since it's been a few weeks now, you might feel comfortable giving me an interview. After all, our viewers are—"

"I told you no before, and it's still no. Now get off of my property and leave me alone!"

He moved toward her. "I understand that you—"

"You understand nothing. Just go away. Go away," she yelled and ran into the house. She slammed the door behind her and took a deep breath to compose herself.

Then with a burst of nervous energy, she went to the kitchen sink where she rinsed and transferred a stack of dirty dishes, glasses, and cups to the dishwasher. She filled the sink with soap and water and wiped down the counter. She carried the sponge to the island, but instead of wiping it, she slid onto a stool and sobbed into her folded arms.

———————

SHE HAD SHUT out everyone in her life except Sandra, who stopped by as often as Melanie would allow. After weeks of watching Melanie suffer, she spoke up.

"Mel, it's time for you to talk to a professional. "I love you, but I can't help you with this. Please." She put a business card on the kitchen counter. "I made an appointment for you on Thursday. I'll pick you up at one o'clock."

Melanie was stubborn, but not stupid. She kept the appointment. Dr. Andrea Stone was a doctor of psychology, not medicine, and about her age. To Melanie's relief, she spoke in soft tones and had a gentle manner. After reviewing Melanie's background and the questionnaire she had filled out, she looked into Melanie's eyes and said, "Tell me how you feel about what's happened."

"Well, how did it go?" Sandra said when Melanie walked back into the waiting room.

"She's okay. I guess I'll come back next week."

A PART OF Scott wanted to see his mother. The other part was relieved that he didn't have to talk to her. They hadn't talked much at the funeral. He hadn't been sure she would attend. But then he knew she always did the "right" thing, and she went through the motions for his sake as well as for public perception.

It had been hard for him, too. The absurdity of it still disturbed him. What exactly is the protocol for burying a father who had held his wife and son hostage during the commission of a murder?

It didn't matter now. What mattered was how to face his friends, family, and the department. He solved that problem by not reaching out to anyone and taking time off work. That tack had seemed to help after suffering the humiliation of Adriana.

A month had passed, and time had quelled some of the sting from the shooting, so he reported to his office. He'd only heard from Charlie once or twice since the incident, but he knew his partner had also taken some days off.

Charlie had arrived earlier and stood up when Scott walked into the room. They greeted each other with a bro-hug.

"How you doing?" Charlie asked first.

"I'm fine. Ready to get back to work."

"You sure?"

"I can't sit home anymore." He motioned toward the files on Charlie's desk. "What have you got?

AFTER FOUR SESSIONS with the therapist, Melanie knew she had to get out of her Valley house. She packed her bags and headed for San Pedro. She walked into the backdoor of McNeil's to the sound of screeching saws and pounding hammers. In her absence, the bar and adjoining living quarters had been completely gutted. She went over to the contractor and tapped him on the shoulder.

"How are things going?"

He removed his ear plugs. "Oh, hi ma'am. Glad you're here. We ran across an issue with the electrical leading from the kitchen into the bar. Looks like we're going to have to re-do it. It's way out of code, and—"

She didn't hear the rest. Her mind had wandered to Benny, and how he would've felt about this guy tearing down his life.

She approved the electrical work and carried her bags up the stairs. The studio hadn't changed since she had lived there in the seventies. The place needed a good cleaning before she could even think about emptying her bags. She considered checking into a hotel, but she couldn't face the stares the publicity about the shooting would generate.

She gathered cleaning supplies from the bar closet and went to work. Almost every space or article she touched elicited a memory; turning eighteen and her father telling her she could move up there, hours dreaming of a singing career, lying in bed with Enzo, and that fateful night with Ted.

Over the next few days, she removed the clutter, scrubbed the room of dirt and grime, and painted the burnt orange walls an ocean blue. Next, she re-arranged the furniture, bought new bedding, and hung inexpensive pictures with inspirational messages. After that, she stood back and admired her handywork. Sometimes going back is a good way to start over.

———

WORKING CASES TOOK Scott's mind off his father. He just wished he didn't have to talk to anyone besides Charlie. The uneasiness among his co-workers in the office was palpable. Some went out of their way to be nice and offer their sympathy, some avoided the subject altogether. But the hardest were the ones that averted their eyes when they spoke or passed him in the hallway.

"Ignore it, kid," Charlie said. "They either don't know what to say, or they're assholes and aren't worth worrying about."

Easy enough for Charlie to say, Scott thought. Even though he'd risked his own skin for him and his mother, Charlie didn't carry the burden of not knowing if he should've been the one to pull the trigger that day, instead of his mother. Either way, it had been the end of the family as Scott knew it. And the reactions of the staff in the office made it impossible to get through the day without it haunting him.

———

AFTER THREE MONTHS of counseling and focusing on the remodel, Melanie began reaching out to Scott. They had dinner a few times, but the conversation was strained and revolved around his work and the bar. She hadn't spoken to Charlie for some time either, so when he called and asked to see her, she invited him to her new digs.

"I heard you moved back here." He sat on her daybed. "Kind of a comedown from your Valley house, isn't it?"

"I needed to re-group, and this seemed like the best place to do it."

"Planning to go back up there?"

She shook her head. "It's on the market."

"I'm glad. It's nice to know you're close by." He smoothed his shirt. "Maybe we can see each other. Go out to dinner, take in a movie."

"I don't think it's a good idea right now. After everything that's happened, I just don't—"

"I get it." He shuffled his feet. "Um, I wanted to talk to you about Scott."

Morbid thoughts ran through her mind. "Is he all right?"

"That's what I came to ask you. He came back to work, saying he had to keep busy, but he's late almost every day and seems to have trouble focusing. His work is shoddy and incomplete, and our cases are falling apart because of it. So far, I've been able to cover for him, but I don't know how long I can keep doing that before the Captain notices."

THE NEXT DAY, Melanie asked Scott to drop by McNeil's to help her with some heavy lifting of furniture she'd ordered for the new club. She tried to ease into a conversation by asking him about his love life.

"Been seeing anyone these days?" she asked.

"No one in particular. Thought I'd play the field for a while."

"That's probably a good thing." She said with a smile. "As long as you're out there."

"And how about you?"

"Me?"

"Sure," he said, his lips twisting into a bitter smile. "You had somebody while Dad was still here. Why not now?"

Melanie had hoped connecting with Scott would allow her to recommend counseling to him. She felt it would help him as it had her. After his biting remark she knew his recent behavior ran deeper than grief, and she'd lost him, along with everything else. She could only hope Charlie would keep him in line while Scott saw his way through this.

CHARLIE POUNDED ON Scott's door. No one answered, but he followed the blaring music to a side window and peeked in it. He rapped on the window, and Scott lifted the curtain. Charlie motioned toward the entrance, walked back, and waited at the door.

Scott opened it a crack. "Charlie?" he said.

Charlie pushed the door open wider and stepped inside, crushing one of the beer cans littering the floor. "What's going on here?"

Scott stood there in jockey shorts and a rumpled T shirt. He ran his fingers through his greasy hair and squinted. "What time is it?"

"It's six o'clock."

"In the morning?"

"Shit, no. Why weren't you at work today?"

"It's Sunday."

"Like hell it is. It's Monday. What's wrong with you? You sick?"

Scott dropped into a chair and rubbed his head. "Yeah, I'm sick."

Charlie looked around the messy room, bent over the coffee table, and picked up two empty bottles of whiskey.

"How long you been holed up in here?"

Scott shrugged. "Friday night, I think."

"Take a shower and get dressed. We're going to go get you some food." They went to an Italian place for dinner. Scott picked at his food, as they sat in silence.

Finally Charlie said, "I've woken up in a cold sweat a couple of times since that day. How about you?"

"You have?"

"Sure. You think I just took that in my stride?"

"I guess I didn't think about it."

"Pretty wrapped up in yourself, huh?"

"It's not every day you're forced to choose whether or not to blow your father away."

Charlie nodded.

"Lucky for you your mother covered you." Charlie took a mouthful of lasagna. "Nothing like a mother's love. Have you talked to her lately?"

"Last week."

"Did you thank her?"

"Thank her? She did it for herself."

"Well, we all had a lot to lose."

"She never loved him, ya know. It was that Mancini guy she wanted. She played my old man for a sucker."

Charlie cleared his throat and wiped his mouth with his napkin. "Well," he said, "there was a lot more to it than that."

CHAPTER 15

MELANIE AND SANDRA sipped wine as they admired the newly remodeled McNeil's.

"This place looks fabulous," Sandra said. "so why haven't you scheduled the grand opening?"

"I don't know if I'm ready to commit to a date yet."

"But you're doing so much better now."

"I'm not sure enough time has passed since Ted's, uh, death."

"What are you afraid of?"

Melanie lowered her head. "People might think I'm capitalizing on what happened."

"Do you think that would stop them from showing up to see the woman behind the headlines? It could be great for business."

"I suppose."

"Come on, Mel. What's the real reason?"

Melanie shrugged. She knew if she told Sandra that after all this time she feared failing, Sandra would say it wouldn't happen. She had always been her biggest supporter. But what if she did bomb? Her dream would turn into a nightmare, and what would she have left?

SCOTT AND CHARLIE had just received a dressing down from the captain after he'd found out that the DA wasn't able to prosecute a case because their evidence had been compromised. The two detectives filed out of the office with heads down. Scott wiped the sweat from his upper lip and followed behind Charlie. He couldn't look at him, but he sensed his anger as they walked out of the station door in silence.

When they reached the car, Charlie ordered, "Get in."

Scott complied, and Charlie drove out of the lot and onto a busy street. A wave of nausea hit Scott and he fidgeted in his seat. It had been his screw up, and he didn't know what to say.

Charlie drove to a local grocery store, parked in the back of the building, and stared out the windshield. "That's the last time I take the heat because of you. I've covered for you as long as I can. I'm too close to retirement to fuck up now."

"I'm sorry, I—"

"I don't want any more of your bullshit excuses." Charlie turned to face him. "You've been through a rough time. I know it, your mother knows it, and despite what you might think, most of the staff in the Bureau knows it. Your father's actions put a stigma on this department, but you don't have to wear it on your back."

Scott pressed his hand to his mouth in an attempt to suppress the tears building behind his eyes.

"Son, it's time to move on. If you can't do it on your own, then go see the department shrink. Either way, you better grow a set of balls, because you're going to need them. You're being transferred to Southeast Division patrol next week, and you'll be too busy protecting your ass from bullets to worry about your emotional problems."

MELANIE HAD BEGUN moving her things downstairs into the fresh new living quarters. She had combined her father's room with the spare room to create one big master suite with the kitchen and office separating it from the bar rooms. It wasn't luxurious, but it gave her more space, and would do until she sold the house and figured out what to do next.

She had just brought down a box when she spotted someone peering into the window of the bar. Walking closer, she recognized Alice from the Chamber of Commerce.

"Hello. Come in," she said as she pushed the door open.

"Hi, Melanie. I've been meaning to call you since Ted's funeral, but wasn't sure where you were."

Melanie motioned her to take a seat in a booth. "I've been here for about a month and just finished the remodel."

Alice waved off the invitation to sit. "I remember talking to you about it that night at the mixer. I've been watching all the activity around here."

Melanie flashed back to that night when she watched Ted drive off without her.

"So when are you going to open?"

"Well, that's on hold."

"Is there a problem?"

"No. Just a matter of me, getting my act together."

"There's a lot of buzz about this club in town, ya know."

"Really? Good or bad?"

"Mostly good."

"What about the bad?"

"Oh, there's always the gossips who enjoy tearing people down. But the business owners are hoping this place will bring new customers to the area. That's the bottom line for them, and me," Alice said and started toward the door.

"Well, I—"

Alice turned back to her. "Listen, I can't tell you how to deal with your personal life, but as one businesswoman to another, I'm telling you, you need to open these doors."

Alice had hit a nerve with her. She made the reason for opening the club more about Melanie's responsibility as a good neighbor than about a personal triumph. That afternoon, Melanie changed into her workout clothes and hit the beach. Running always helped her think.

When she returned home, she called Sandra to tell her she had decided to set a date for the grand opening. They agreed to brainstorm the plans the next day. Later on, she took a shower and dressed. There was somebody she needed to tell in person.

SHE CLIMBED THE steps to the small Spanish bungalow and gave the door knocker a few taps. When no one answered, she shifted from one foot to the other. I guess I should've called, she thought, and took a step down off the stoop. The door flew open, and she turned around to face Charlie.

"Melanie," he said with surprise.

She stepped back up. "Hey."

"Come on in. Everything okay?"

She stepped inside. "Yeah."

"Haven't talked to you for a while. How are you doing?" He pointed to the couch for her to sit.

"I'm all right. Much better, actually." She sat down.

"So, you here to talk about Scott's transfer? I'm sure you—"

"It's not about Scott. I'm his mother, and I don't like him working the south end, but if he can stay safe, I think it might help him right now."

He plopped down onto a chair. "Then what's on your mind?"

"I'm announcing the grand opening of the club this week. It'll be in about six weeks."

"Scott told me you were dragging your feet about that. What changed your mind?"

"Something one of the local business owners said to me. Made me realize it's the right thing to do."

"Of course it is. It's been your dream for a long time."

"I know, but after so much had happened, I had second thoughts." He nodded.

"I had second thoughts about a lot of things." she said. "Therapy does that to you."

"I wouldn't know. I've avoided it for a long time."

"Well, let me tell you, it's not for the faint of heart. It can be pretty brutal coming face to face with the things you've spent years denying. And there were a lot of things. But one in particular bothered me the most. It's that regardless of how I treated you over the years, I can't deny that I've always loved you and want you more than I've ever wanted anyone."

Charlie responded with silence, as if trying to let what she had said sink in.

She couldn't read him. "Well, uh." She started to rise, but Charlie sprang from his chair, put his arms around her, and caressed her face with his lips.

She welcomed his kisses as she had that night on the beach, but this time she allowed herself to experience the sensations that came with them. He lifted her top and nuzzled her chest, and she pulled him tighter to her. It had been a long time, and yet it seemed natural when he took her hand and led her into his bed, where he unfastened her bra.

As he waited for her to remove it, a chill came over her, and she hesitated; aware of how her body had not weathered the years as well as her emotions had. What if they couldn't re-create their erotic fantasies of the past? She thought. What if—?

He must have realized her feelings. "We've waited this long," he said. "We can take a little more time." Then he wrapped his arms around her and pulled her down on the bed with him, where they spent the rest of the afternoon talking and fondling, before consummating their long deferred desires.

SCOTT HAD BEEN assigned to days at Southeast Division, seventeen miles northeast of San Pedro. About ten square miles located in south central Los Angeles, the area was known for its crime and notorious gang activity. Traffic on his first day was a bitch from San Pedro, but working in the daylight would help him get accustomed to the area. Besides, days were generally not as busy as nights.

Having taken Charlie's advice, Scott had had a round of sessions with the department psychologist before arriving at his new assignment. One of the subjects that had come up, addressed the reason Scott had become a cop in the first place. Had he been coerced to join the force?

Growing up a cop's son meant that higher standards would be imposed on him by his parent. After all, a child of an officer should never exhibit signs of the sleazy element he/she faced in the street every day. The offshoot of this often resulted in a rebellious child determined to defy the pressure placed on him to be perfect, often creating the opposite effect; the drug addict, school drop-out, or criminal. In Scott's case, he strived to make his father proud of him by emulating him. Which meant joining the force.

The counselor had recommended that he consider his life as a civilian. What did he envision himself doing other than police work? He took a sober look at what his life would be without the job he had come to love. His decision had led him to Southeast station that day.

He arrived early, despite the traffic, and pulled into the parking lot. He noticed a few other people, but made no eye contact with them. He slung his gun belt over his shoulder, retrieved his uniform and duffle bag from the backseat and walked around to the front of the station. The civilian desk officer showed him into an office, and introduced him to Capt. Morales, sitting at his desk.

"Have a seat." Morales pointed to a chair.

Scott complied, and did his best to act nonchalant, as the muscles on his arms twitched under his lightweight jacket. He told himself that he shouldn't be nervous. After all, he'd just left a special assignment with South Bureau Homicide and had worked patrol for more than two years. But it wasn't lack of experience that concerned him.

The captain wasted no time before addressing Scott's fears. "I was sorry to hear about the circumstances of your father's death. Ted and I came on the job about the same time. He was a good cop back then; a good partner."

Scott could see the disappointment on the man's face.

Morales took a deep breath and walked to the front of his desk. "I realize you have taken the brunt of this situation, and I admire your determination to continue with the department, despite recent problems at your last assignment. But if you're serious about working here, you're going to have to find a way to get beyond your unfortunate family issues, and re-commit yourself to the job. Your fellow officers' and the community's lives depend on it. "

SCOTT LEFT THE captain's office relieved. Though he knew he had more work ahead of him to get where he could reconcile his feelings about his parents' actions, he felt up to the challenge that the captain had just given him. As Scott entered the locker room he interrupted the conversation of three other officers. He nodded to them and they returned the gesture but continued their business in silence.

He located his assigned number, hung his gun belt inside the locker door, and tucked his duffle bag on the shelf. After ripping open the plastic cleaning bag over his blue uniform, he undressed. The quiet in the room spoke volumes, so Scott hurriedly strapped on his bullet-proof vest before donning the rest of his uniform.

At roll call, the sergeant introduced him to mixed responses. Scott chose to focus on the openly positive ones and was grateful to be partnered with Ken Kawaguchi, a veteran of the division. Ken offered to drive, and when they hit the streets, he filled Scott in on their area of assignment. Scott had been away from patrol for a while but had no problem remembering the routine. He also discovered that he had missed the self-confidence and sense of importance that wearing the uniform gave him.

Ken cruised around the streets, pointing out some of the troublesome areas. Afterward, they bought an indecent exposure call of a man wagging his penis at some children in the park, and then went on to file a report of a liquor store theft. The relatively simple reports gave Scott time to get familiar with the area and learn about the ever-present gang problems in the hood.

It was getting close to lunch time, so Scott picked up the microphone and requested code 7 from the RTO.

"18A35 continue patrol," she responded. "415 man with a gun, 146 E. 111th St., shots fired. Code3."

Scott acknowledged the call, and Ken hit the red lights and siren and floored the gas pedal. They pulled up in front of a wood-framed bungalow, eased out of the car with guns drawn, and called out to the suspect inside the house. The man responded with a barrage of gunfire.

"Shit!" Ken said as they took cover behind the car doors.

Scott's voice shook when he spoke into the microphone attached to his shirt. "18A35. Officer needs help. Shots fired at police. We have a barricaded suspect. Requesting additional units, a supervisor and an air unit."

Still crouching, he thought about his next move, while wondering what had driven the man to this point. Was he guilty of another crime and determined not to go to jail, or was he a despondent man on drugs, hoping to commit suicide by cop? Either way, Scott knew the odds of this confrontation ending well were slim to none.

Before the RTO finished announcing that the officers needed help, two additional police units pulled up along with Air Support Unit3, having heard the original hot shot call earlier. Ken directed them to position themselves at the rear and sides of the house, and Air3, circling above the neighborhood, confirmed that they had seen no one exit the back.

Within minutes, Sgt. Hillary Sanders arrived, followed by four more black and whites. Scott apprised the sergeant of the situation, and she requested a SWAT team. She used the extra officers to help her set up a command post a few houses away, manage the news media and other bystanders, and close the street at both ends.

In the meantime, Scott took it upon himself to canvass the neighbors for information about the suspect. Two neighbors were not home, and another claimed to know nothing about the shooter. He finally found an older woman willing to help.

"That man's a funny one. Doesn't have much to say and when he does, it never makes sense. He lives with his sister. She's a nice lady.

Quiet. Belongs to my church."

"Uh, you don't happen to have her phone number, do you?"

"Wait here. I'll check my church roster."

Scott nodded. If he could get the number, they might be able to call the house, talk to the guy and find out if anyone else was in there.

"Here you go." She handed him a slip of paper with the number.

"Thank you, ma'am."

He took the information back to Sgt. Sanders.

"Good job Swain." she said, looking him directly in the eye.

Scott went back to his car and resumed his position with Ken. Until then, he had been operating on adrenaline, and although the incident was far from over, her simple expression of approval plus knowing that SWAT had arrived, lessened the tension.

Meanwhile, Sgt. Sanders called the phone number that Scott had obtained. When there was no answer, she flipped on a car speaker. "This is Sgt. Sanders of the LAPD. Speaking to all persons at 146 E. 111th St. I'm ordering you to immediately come out the front door with your hands raised." After repeating the command three times, to no avail, she informed her officers to remain at their posts, and wait for SWAT to suit up and deploy in the area.

Once SWAT officers surveyed the residence and positioned themselves around the perimeter and on the roof across the street, they launched a canister of tear gas into the house. The fumes from the gas permeated the street and scorched Scott's face, forcing him to close his tearing eyes. When he opened them again, Ken's face was a blur. The white substance hung in the air as they waited for someone to run out of the house. No one did.

SWAT officers then rammed the door to enter the house with guns prepared to blaze. A few minutes later, the SWAT supervisor stepped out of the house and announced that the scene was clear.

Scott and Ken had to see for themselves. They entered the living room to find an overweight man in his thirties sprawled on the couch, gun next to him, with blood and matter oozing from his head.

"Sorry son of a bitch," Ken said.

After making their way into the kitchen, they spotted a lifeless middle-aged woman with a gunshot wound in her chest, slumped in a chair at the table. Scott winced, as he stood over her body, remembering her neighbor's description of the "nice lady."

Ken glanced over at Scott. "Well, partner, welcome to life in Watts."

CHAPTER 16

MELANIE STRAIGHTENED HER long black gown and put the finishing touches on her hair and make-up as she readied for the long-awaited grand opening of McNeil's. She'd been going since early morning, taking care of last minute preparations in the kitchen and the bar. She grabbed the can of hairspray, and heard a tap on the door. She turned to see Charlie, looking quite dapper in the tux he had rented for her special occasion.

"Hey, Mel. Wow, you look beautiful." He leaned in to brush her cheek with his lips.

She pretended to straighten his bow tie. "You're pretty handsome yourself." Handing him her diamond necklace, she turned and waited for him to fasten it around her neck.

"You ready for this?"

She drew a long breath. "As ready as I'll ever be, I guess."

"You're going to be great."

The evening was by invitation only for chamber members, and friends and family, with limited reservations for the public. Cocktails and appetizers began at six with dinner planned for eight. Even though she had hired the best up-and-coming chef in the area, along with experienced bartenders and servers, she still worried about her new staff's maiden dinner.

On top of that, it would also be her first appearance as a singer in a very long time. So much was riding on this evening. It had to be great. But that wasn't her only concern. She hadn't received an RSVP from Scott, and if he didn't show, no matter how successful the party was, she would be crushed.

A FEW MINUTES past seven, Scott arrived with a stunning statuesque young woman on his arm. He quickly spotted Charlie and meandered over to him.

"Hey, Charlie." Scott said.

Charlie straightened his stance, and tipped his drink at Scott. "Good to see you. Your mother will be pleased. Kind of kept her guessing, though."

"Yeah. I didn't mean to. I just needed some time."

Charlie nodded. "So introduce us."

"Oh, Shelley. This is Charlie Moore my former partner at South Bureau. And a good friend of my Mom."

"Nice to meet you." The shapely blonde held out her hand. "Pleasure's mine."

Scott scanned the crowded room. "Mom around?"

"Think she's in the kitchen. Hey, I read about that shooting caper of yours at Southeast. Good job."

"Thanks, it was hairy."

"Thought it stunk that they led the story with Ted's shooting, though. Goddamn media."

Scott had been trying to forget that story in the news. It probably wouldn't have made it on TV if it hadn't given them another chance to use his father's name. Anything for a headline. He needed to change the subject. "Uh, they keeping you busy at the Bureau?"

"Sure. For the time being. Maybe you didn't hear. I'm pulling the pin next month."

Scott smiled. "So you're finally packing it in for a life of leisure?"

"Matter of fact, no. I took a job as a DA investigator with the county. I start in a couple of months."

"You're kidding. Why the switch?"

Turns out my finances weren't good enough for me to live on retirement alone. But I needed a change. Thirty years with the PD was enough.

"Well, the DA's the winner as far as I'm concerned." Scott turned to Shelley. "Come on, let's go find Mom."

THE EVENING DIDN'T go without its hiccups, but the overall reception by the guests was encouraging. They loved everything from the art deco black and yellow décor to the cuisine. Everyone appreciated that she had restored Benny's bar counter, complete with some of the etched names, and added a tastefully done collage of Benny's personal mementoes, pictures, and awards. Melanie became wrapped in his spirit as she pictured her father standing proudly behind the bar winking at her.

Her song set, though the most unnerving part of the evening, became the highlight for her as she found her voice and conveyed her well-deserved peace of mind after a year of trauma, loss, and recovery. And to top it off, Scott was there with her. Whenever she looked over at him during the evening, he was fully engaged in the event, taking pride in his mother's accomplishment.

Maybe I've finally earned my son's respect again, she thought. We might just have survived the worst time of our lives.

Made in the USA
Las Vegas, NV
27 June 2021

25544084R00090